Revenge Of The Damned (The Montana Series)

by

L.J. Martin

WOLFPACK
PUBLISHING

Print Edition
© Copyright 2017 L.J. Martin

Wolfpack Publishing

P.O. Box 620427
Las Vegas, NV 89162

All rights reserved. No part of this book may be reproduced by any means without the prior written consent of the publisher, other than brief quotes for reviews.

ISBN: 978-1-62918-743-3

Revenge of the Damned
(The Montana Series)

by

L.J. Martin

A special thanks to two gentlemen with incisive red pens....

John Corbin

And my fellow creeker... Ron Clausen

Chapter One

DAMNED IF THERE'S TIMES when a cup full of blood don't look like a slop bucket full. I hope this is one of those times.

'Cause if it ain't, I'm about bled out.

When there's been a half-dozen owlhoots slinging lead your way, one of them's bound to get lucky, and damned if one of them didn't. Maybe two. I'm shot through and through the side, thank the good Lord below the ribs and above the hip bone. Unless the side wound clipped a gut, they didn't get any vitals.

Unless....

But I won't be sitting easy for a while as a big slug done knocked a chunk outta the bottom of my thigh, which is likely the one what killed my horse right out from under me.

Damn fine horse, old Blue. If I live, I'll get a pound or two of flesh from them what did him in. If I live. And I'm missing my hound as well. If they killed Scout...well...I'll do my best to make sure them what put us all in a bad way, dies slow.

If'n I hadn't pulled my Golden Boy as old Blue went down, and took up a position behind him, dropping one of my pursuers off'n his horse, and the horse out from under another, I'd likely be hanging from the closest cottonwood tree. For they scattered into the alleys like quail from a hound dog rather

Revenge of the Damned

than charging me with their superior numbers. But I hated unhorsing the one I did, as I was shooting at the City Marshal, who I know needed killing. I can only hope the deputy was a low life as well, and not some storekeeper trying to do his civic duty.

As it is, odds are, without a sawbones at hand, one or both of these holes in me is likely to go green, and that will be that. It'll take a while, a good, long, stinkin' while and I'll be tempted to try the taste of my own gun barrel if it gets too terrible to go on.

Old Blue in the middle of the road, five fellas still trying to work my way, and as God provides there was a hitching rail full of horseflesh only steps away. I picked a good one who looked like he could run...and added horse thief to deputy slayer.

Another "thank-you-Lord" was the fact I had a flint and steel in a pocket or this cave would for sure be a cold grave, got a fire built, and now have my Arkansas toothpick heating to red on the tip. Since there ain't no pretty split-tail in the neighborhood to sew me up, it'll have to be scorch and scream to get the blood to quit messin' the hard-packed bone-and-guano littered floor of this cave. If I don't pass out while it's heatin' up, or with the first stench of burned flesh, I might live to see the light of a new day. Normally that smell wouldn't offend me to that state, passin' out, but when it's your own burned flesh it may be a different matter.

I smelled plenty of it in the war, mostly cannon fodder, but none of it my own.

Finding this cave was pure luck; finding dry wood inside, out of the rain, was providence. Now if those on my tail don't see or smell the wood smoke or burned flesh and ferret me out.... Well that'll be one of them miracles Jesus gained his reputation from gettin' done. Maybe not quite that, but close enough to suit this cowhand, wrangler, saddle-maker, soldier.

And cuckolder—if that's a proper word for the one doin' the deed and not being the cuckold—as former Colonel and now Marshal Oscar Wentworth would say. And for good reason, as it was his wife, and my hunger, was the cause of this whole affair. That, and a lie. Then again, had I not accepted the invitation of a woman looking you right in the eye and saying what a lying no good son-of-a-bitch her husband was, then me, old Blue, and Scout would likely be ambling down the trail heading south to Wyoming and on into Kansas or over the divide into Utah and Nevada before snow flies. Our biggest worry would be the occasional rabbit, grouse or sage hen to drop for supper, or the rain turning to white snow. Not my own flesh going to stinking green rot.

Why did she say that about her own lawfully wedded husband? Then drag me down on my mattress? 'Cause he lied to her, that's why. Looked her right in her pretty blue eyes and told her he'd seen me killed on the battlefield, and who wouldn't believe an officer and a gentleman? That would be me who wouldn't, and his woman for a short time, that's who. Of course Wentworth, or Wentworthless as those of us who served under him came to call him, didn't seem to much care what we believed. Or what he said or did in order to get his way.

And he earned the scorn of his troop.

Not only that, but we were sure he was a no-good thief, as three months of our pay went missing while under his care. He claimed a deserter had it and was long gone. None of us believed him, but all of us were sick of the killing and just wanted to go home...even with empty pockets.

I'm sorta glad he did lie to her, as Maggie Mae paid him with more scorn by serving under me for a short while. Fact was I enjoyed not only the long overdue act, but almost as much the fact it was the wife of Wentworthless. The hell of it was, it got her shot dead.

Fact was I knew Maggie Mae before I went off to war, and thought she was promised to me.

And she thought so too, until I died...or so she was led to believe.

Revenge of the Damned

After the news of Appomattox came through, when I finally walked my way from Hannibal, Missouri to Helena, Montana, she'd done married Wentworth—who, being an officer, had a train and stage voucher and beat me home by three months—and I kept going without even confronting her and asking why. When I finally returned this ten years later, and run into my old flame in the Cattlemen's Club where she confronted me while Wentworth was out in the privy, we both learned the truth.

And the truth hurt me clean to the core, and I guess her too, as I was to discover.

It was only a day later, yesterday, that she showed up at my Cattlemen's Club hotel door, brazen as a Cantina floozy, and we sealed our fate.

At least hers, as Wentworth shot her dead that very night, only knowing she'd been seen going up the hotel stairs. Enough of an offense in his eyes as there were only men in residence there. And soon as I heard the fact of his heinous act, later in the Cattlemen's saloon, I said then and there that I was going to shoot him dead. I was sure he'd be coming after me when he found out I was staying at the hotel and knowing of our former relationship. And it didn't take long for him to learn my whereabouts, and put two and two together.

My own fault.

One should not speak in anger, announcing his intentions to all the world and a saloon full of strangers with one's eyes full of tears, no matter how much one might mean what one says. Some liver-lip in the crowd, who witnessed my outburst, got to Marshal Wentworthless and warned him. Him and six of his deputies—four of them volunteers as I knew he had only two on the payroll—came marching down the middle of Last Chance Gulch. So, discretion being the better part of valor, I figured I'd bide my time for revenge and lit out for the hostler and saddled up...not quite fast enough as they lay down on me with long arms as I raised dust heading out of the livery.

Glancing down I see the tip of my pig sticker is glowing red. This is going to be a troika of hurt, as I have an in and out on my side and a still bleeding hole where the chunk was blown out of my thigh. I grab a hard thumb-thick branch and clamp my teeth around it. Having to do the back by feel, I pray I hit the spot on the first go. I must have hit something, as the two handfuls of goober peanuts I downed with my beers in the Cattlemen's come up and damn near put out my little fire. My head swims and I lay back for a second, but only a second as I lay on the blistering wound and lurch back upright.

"One down," I say aloud, with some hoopla I don't truly feel, and it echoes up the cave. The knife goes back in the fire to redden again, sizzling with the blood now covering it, while I fight the nausea.

My mouth has gone dry as a dust devil, and I realize I have no water. Which is a hell of a note as I rode through an inch of rain getting here. That will limit my time in the cave, if the damn cauterizing don't kill me dead first.

If so, I'll be here until the coyotes find me.

Chapter Two

"WELL, TWODOGS, WHICH WAY?" Marshal Wentworth demanded from his Crow tracker.

The stoic Indian, now dismounted, glanced up from studying the tracks in the mud. He knew that even an idiot could follow this trail, but still acted as if he was having to work hard to do so. The man—Lincoln Dolan he'd been told—had kept his mount in the stream, against the current, for a quarter mile until he was faced with a six-foot waterfall. It was plain as the scream of a hawk where he'd left the stream bed onto a wide sweep of rounded river rock. Even with no imprints in mud, the scraping of iron shoes on the mossy rocks could be tracked by his five year old son.

They'd been on the trail since the first hint of dawn, which was unusual for the fat Marshal. He normally didn't rise until long after the rooster crowed. But he was angry, and Twodogs was amused. It was said this man, Dolan, had taken the Marshal's woman. Why these white eyes were driven to insanity by a few minutes of their woman's time given to another man was beyond him, but he'd seen it before. It wasn't like the woman was being used by her husband at the time.

He could care less about the way of it, only about the gold double eagle he'd been promised if he tracked Dolan down. And he would do so, if only this fat Marshal and his five deputies could keep up. Even on foot, leading his own mount, he continually left them behind.

He followed the trail on up the rocky slope for a hundred yards, leaving nary a track with his own moccasins until it all but disappeared onto a fifty-pace wide rock ledge that ended in an escarpment that rose two or three hundred feet above. The base of the cliff was lined by a thick line of chokecherry that occluded the crotch where ledge met cliff. Probably a wet spot for the hundred-pace length of the tree thicket as the rain and even dew collecting on the cliff would pool at that bottom juncture.

Twodogs was suspicious as he wondered if Dolan hadn't doubled back, carefully retracing his steps to again enter the stream above the falls.

He'd found a few drops of blood from time to time, knowing the man was wounded. He also knew a wounded man or animal got very cagey, knowing that his every move must be carefully thought out or it might be his last.

Then again, as the Crow tracker neared the twenty-foot-deep copse of chokecherry, he wondered if the man were merely hiding in the thicket, and might have a rifle leveled on him right now. Acting more casual than he felt, he yawned, stretching his arms wide, then turned and headed back where the posse, forty yards behind, was just moving up the ledge to join him.

It wouldn't do to have Dolan think he was excited about closing in on him. If so, the hunted man might get reckless.

"You damn fool, did you lose him?" Wentworth snapped.

Unblinking, Twodogs stared at the man for a long moment. He'd lifted hair for less of an insult. In a quiet tone, he spoke. "Twodogs no fool. Dolan may be in thicket, he may not be. See no horse, so need to work rock until I find where he went. You white eye fools move horses back. Hard to tell one horseshoe from next."

"Careful, Twodogs," Wentworth said. "You're not leading a war party any longer, and no one would give a damn I left you to rot on this ledge."

Revenge of the Damned

Twodogs merely glared at him for a moment, then repeated, "Move horses back."

Wentworth spun his horse and waved to his men. "Let's water the horses while the red nigger hunts the trail."

Twodogs knew that, too, was an insult. And wondered if maybe he'd lift the fat Marshal's hair when this was over. He'd liked the Marshal's woman, as she was respectful and had even fed him a time or two, taking the food outside to him as Wentworth wouldn't allow him in the house. And Wentworth had sent the woman to wherever the souls of the white eyes went. She was a good woman, and Wentworth was not fit to share her teepee. There would be a time.

He ground tied his horse and moved carefully along the edge of the chokecherries, slowly he studied each rock and crevice, and every pathway into the trees looking for tracks or broken branches.

After several minutes, he looked up to see Wentworth gigging his horse his way again. He moved down the ledge, away from where the tale of the escaping man was told.

Wentworth shouted at him from halfway up the rock to rejoin him. "Damn you, Twodogs, what the hell are you doing?"

"Horse moved on up stream, but I think man not on him."

"Then where the hell's the man?"

"Probably watching you from trees, ready to blow head off."

Wentworth involuntarily ducked, which made Twodogs smile, then call after him as the Marshal gave his horse spurs and stayed low in the saddle as he rejoined his men. "Go water horse."

Twodogs backtracked, wondering where and why the man had abandoned his mount, if in fact he had, then after a couple of dozen steps, saw the telltale broken branches where the man, or a deer or elk, had pushed its way into the thick trees.

The Indian stood and studied the cliff face through the heavy branches, shading his eyes, letting them adjust to the

8

darkness. After a moment he made out where the grass was flattened and a two-foot high indentation was deeply shadowed, and small tracks showed animals had been passing in and out of the wide but low hole.

Could it be a cave, and was the man there?

Chapter Three

I AWOKE WHEN THE LOW narrow opening of the cave, which faced southeast, began to lighten. Damn, I'm sore, and stiff, but, thank God, not feverish. My wounds shout at me with every movement, but they don't weep puss. If I can only stay away from my wounds going green, I have a chance. I've managed to cauterize all, and the bleeding has stopped, but how long will it stay stopped.

My tongue is so dry I wonder if that very necessary appendage might crack off, and know I have to have water. So, I begin to edge my way the twenty feet or so back to the opening. It takes all of fifteen minutes as I have to keep from dragging a damn wound and have them both front and back, but painfully, I make it.

There is no trickle of water to be seen, and working my way most of a hundred yards down to the creek is out of the question. However, there's lots of dew and even some frost on the leaves of the chokecherries, and patiently, slowly, I strip the leaves into my hand until I have an eighth inch of water, then suck it down and start the process over again. Then I realize the tiny cherries themselves, the ones the birds have yet to get, have some moisture and maybe even some nourishment.

So, I eat and drink for at least three hours, wondering even then if I've managed a cup of water. At least my mouth no longer feels like dried horse apples or tastes like the bats that I know must live in the cave because they have deposited their guano there.

As I start inching my way back into the cave, I hear the shouts of men. Several men. And know it must be a posse.

The knot in my gut now suddenly hurts more than my wounds.

I'd earlier loosened the latigo on the horse, stripped the blanket out from under, and dropped the bridle off, dragging it and the blanket into the cave with me. Sure that the saddle would eventually work loose, I'd slapped the dun on the butt and sent him on. He wasn't up to dragging the saddle, and it would be a sure sign of his presence if it lay outside, so it had to go with the horse. Now, if only the damn posse would follow the dun, and if only the horse kept moving along and didn't get hung up and tangled with the saddle in some damn thicket.

If only....

With the increased light in the opening and the low light of my fire, I realize the cave walls are covered with rudimentary pictures. I've seen them on cliff walls before, pictographs I think some call them.

But this is no time to admire aboriginal art.

I manage to throw loose soil on the fire. Then dragging my Golden Boy and my body, I use my good leg and push myself deeper and deeper into the cave, climbing a foot in ten, until, after what seems fifty yards, it is dark as two feet up a buffalo's butt. Then, exhausted, every bone aching, I have to rest.

I know the cave goes somewhere as I've realized the smoke from my fire didn't fill the cave down to the level of the entry, but rather seemed to go deeper, dissipating into the darkness.

But it doesn't mean much...smoke can sure as hell go where a man can't.

I wait where I am, wiggling my butt down into the rocks like a hen warming her eggs, wondering if Wentworth or any of his deputies have the cojones to follow a man with a rifle. A man who's already dropped one of them and another's horse.

Revenge of the Damned

Follow him into a dark hole in the earth? I know damn well I'd think twice about filling a hole with the sun at my back and nothing but darkness ahead. Wentworth only had two full time deputies, so at least some of those who've come to arrest me are townspeople deputized special.

They'll want to go back to selling flour and sugar or cutting hair and shaving faces, or whatever. They'll sure as hell want to go back to their wife and young'uns.

It isn't long before a voice rings out from back where I'd been, and it's a weird echoing sound as it bounces off the walls deep into the cave.

"Come on out, Dolan. You'll get a fair trial."

I remain silent.

"Dolan, I know you're in there. We'll just build a hell of a fire here and smoke you out or cook you like a pot roast, or maybe bring the rocks down from above and seal you in this here tomb you done chose for yourself. You might as well come on out and face up to what you done."

I can't stand it any longer. "And you, Oscar? You gonna stand trial for murdering that woman who was too damn good for you? And for me, for that matter."

"You're damn sure wounded, Dolan. We'll get you back to the doc, should you come on out."

"So he can patch me up and you can hang me?"

"Not without a fair trial."

I manage a laugh, then say, "Here's what I think of your fair trial." I cock and shoulder the Golden Boy and put one near center down the cave. The sound is horrendous, deadening my ear drums for a moment.

When my hearing returns I catch the end of Wentworth's yell, "...and your bloody ma and pa. That cooks it, butt hole. We'll see how you like living in a tomb."

It's quiet for a long spell, then I catch the rattle and crack of rocks falling down the slope above and rattling and stacking up in front of the small opening, and it goes dark. The kind of black that makes one wonder if he might be dead. It sounds as if half the mountain has come down, sealing me like a pharaoh in an Egyptian tomb.

Damn him, I think, it might get real lonely in here, less I can follow the smoke or the bats or some damn thing. And now I have no choice.

I have to keep moving deeper, and deeper, and God forbid, I come to a place where I cannot pass.

Right now, I thought, I'm a little on the tired side so I believe I'll catch a little shut eye. One thing good about this, I won't have to worry about them ol' boys outside sneaking up on me whilst I doze.

Chapter Four

"HERE'S YOUR TEN DOLLARS," Wentworth said, handing Twodogs a gold piece.

"You say twenty," Twodogs replied, giving him a hard stare.

"The hell I did. I said twenty if you track him down. You tracked us to him, maybe, if that was him at all. I got no "shot-full-a-holes" body to show off to town folks, just a story of some owlhoot in a black hole that we never put eyes on. So, that ain't tracking him down. Take this ten and be happy it's not a kick in the butt."

Twodogs stared at him a moment, again without blinking, and finally reached out and took the gold piece.

"Humph," Wentworth said, as his men chuckled. He gave his back to the Indian and walked to his fifteen hand black stud, mounted, and spurred him away. His deputies hooted and hollered as they headed back toward Helena. It was a ten-mile ride, and they'll work up a big hunger and bigger thirst by the time they reach the Cattlemen's Saloon.

Twodogs merely watched them ride away. He turned and looked at the ten-foot width of rocks now covering the cave opening, some of them as big as a rain barrel. When he and two of the deputies had climbed a hundred feet up the steep escarpment and started rocks rolling, they'd been surprised at how the avalanche grew.

Even as big as Twodogs was, he merely stared at the rock pile after the Marshal and deputies rode out of sight. He considered trying to dig his way back to the opening, but then decided he couldn't move several of the boulders without a pair of braves to help. The man was worth another ten dollars, he figured, but there was no way to get to him.

And who was stupid enough to chase a rattlesnake down a hole?

He also considered getting ahead of the posse and finding a good spot to lay in wait and use his well-worn 66 Winchester to put the cheating Marshal down so the worms would have something to feed on. But there were five men with him, and it would be risky. All things in their time, and the time to send the Marshal to what the white eyes called hell, could wait.

He would settle his debt with the Marshal his way, and maybe with a couple of the others who'd laughed when the Marshal cheated him. Maybe that was the white eye way; it wasn't the Crow way.

He recovered his mount and swung up into the saddle he'd rebuilt from one of the McClellan's he'd found on a dead soldier-horse, recovering its frayed and bullet creased forks, cantle, and fenders, with elk hide and decorating the light skin with his own hand prints, dipped in an ochre color. Before he reined away to head back to town, he caught a flash of movement up the mountain side, on the far side of the creek. He sat dead still, watching into a stand of lodge pole pine, until again he saw something move. Then he realized it was a horse, head down, grazing.

He let his paint mustang pick its way down the ledge and gave him the heels to move him over the creek, then up the escarpment on the far side. It was a little rough going until rock pile became soil and brush, then copse of trees.

The dun horse wore a saddle, but it was upside down, hanging loosely under the animal, with no bridle. Twodogs dismounted, untied his own braided lead rope and let his paint drop his head to graze, then made his way casually through the trees with the rope held behind his back. The dun didn't move, other than graze, and let him approach.

He slowly slipped the rope around the dun's neck then tied him to a pine, then sat the saddle back in place and, even though there was no blanket, tightened the latigo.

He did not have a second ten-dollar gold piece but now had a fifty-dollar dun and a five dollar saddle. That would do for the time being.

Now, if he just had the man.

He wondered if the cave had only one entrance. Many, he knew, had more than one and some many.

In no hurry to return to the town the white eyes called Helena, other than an itch to steal a bottle of whiskey, he decided to camp near the creek, kill a whitetail and smoke it, maybe trap a few trout, and wait and watch.

One thing the plains had taught the dozens of generations before him, and had been taught him, was patience.

Chapter Five

IT'S A STRANGE SENSATION to awake in absolute darkness coupled with bone chilling cold. It's too grave-like, which encourages me to try and move. When I had the fire and my space was fairly contained in a ten-foot-wide by seven foot high space, the cold was not so noticeable, but lying flat on cold rock for some time—I have no idea how much time—is numbing. In pure putrid, near freezing, darkness, there is no way to gauge time.

I work my shoulders and stretch my good leg, then feel under my linsey Woolsey shirt to see if there is fresh blood. Thank God, none. And if there is any fever, it's too damn cold to notice.

When I'd dragged the horse blanket and reins in I was only trying to fool my pursuers as to my location, but the blanket has been a godsend. I work my way to standing, only to crack my head on the low roof. Rubbing it off, I move deeper, sure that, behind me, the entrance is well blocked if the roar of falling rock were any indication.

And I promptly bump my forehead. Feeling up and down the obstacle I realize it is a stalactite. I work around it and keep moving, like the blind man I am in the blackness, with both hands extended. After another two hundred paces, always climbing—If you can call my half-step and drag a pace—the ceiling rises away farther than I can reach. I am very, very careful moving, as I have no idea if the floor might fall away and I could be stepping into nothingness.

Then I whoop, so loud the echoes of my own voice frighten me. I say a short prayer of thanks, without kneeling, as kneeling might open my leg wound.

There is a shaft of light up ahead.

That's the good news, the possible bad is it's a good hundred feet from where I lean on the slimy cave wall and the light, that the beams reflect on water. A pool of water which I have no idea the length or width of, and the shaft of light seems to disappear into its depths. It sure as hell isn't a puddle. Then I smile remembering a lieutenant who laughed at me when I balked at crossing a river. I'd said, "It must be fifty feet deep." And the lieutenant had replied, "Sargeant, it don't make a hoot how deep she is, as anything over about six feet means we all swim or drown. Don't matter if'n there's no bottom till China."

And he was right. If you gotta swim you can swim in three feet or a hundred and three. And either one can, sure as hell is hot, drown you.

Of course, back then, I didn't have wounds I had to worry about soaking open.

If it isn't one damn thing it's another damn thing, only this damn thing just might kill me.

I wonder if there is any way I can tell what time of day it might be, then I realize the shafts of light, looking bright enough to be direct sun, are slanted at a forty-five degree angle. I surmise it is either mid-morning or mid-afternoon.

It should give me time to paddle the pool and climb out, if there is a way to climb out. If there truly is a God above, there will be.

I think about discarding the blanket and bridle, but something tells me it would be foolish. Fall is on the land and if I get out of this hell hole it could turn deathly cold. There is no question but that I have to hang onto my Golden Boy.

Tying the blanket around my shoulders with the rifle therein and wrapping the reins around my left arm and binding them in place, I ease into the water. I wish I could keep my wounds from getting wet, but there is no possibility. I'm able to walk a quarter of the way, and have high hopes of walking all the way across, keeping at least the wounds in my side dry, when my feet slip out from under me and I find myself dunked, coughing, then swimming. I'm stroking mostly with my right arm. Every stroke pains me almost to the point of gasping, but soon I find myself passing through the shaft of light, half way to the far side. I try to put my feet down as I'm nearing the far bank, but there is no bottom and I only accomplish getting a choking mouthful of water. I have to cough and cough, but then am able to go on.

A narrow ledge greets me and I'm able to pull myself partially out of the water and lay, gasping, slowing my breathing. I'm fighting nausea from the pain, but calm myself, accept it, and consequently can rest. But it is no place to truly rest as I'm still in a couple of inches of water.

Another goal obtained. I'm not out, I have more light to go by, and can see a spot of sky. Unfortunately, it is fifty or sixty feet above where I rest, at the top of a narrow cleft. It leads up at an angle, but a steep angle. They're maybe handholds, maybe even ledges, as there are dark recesses. Only fifty or sixty feet.

The way I feel at the moment—weak, wounded, cold to the marrow—it might as well be a mile.

Finally, deciding I feel as good as I'll feel until I get dry and something in my gut, I start climbing. I push with my good leg, pulling with my right arm, resting and repeating the process.

I've covered maybe a third of the way, twenty feet in as many minutes.

Then...the rattle of a snake in the narrow shaft sounds like the Transcontinental is about to run me over.

It has to be close, but I can't see the reptile. And my mouth tastes of copper fear.

Chapter Six

TWODOGS ALWAYS CARRIED fishing line with him, just a few feet of braided line, but not usually for fishing.

He'd bent a willow branch and made a snare where little critters were using a path through the willows down to the creek, and he awakened to a rustling in the brush.

Moving stealthily he worked his way through the willows to his snare and the fat snowshoe rabbit trying desperately to free himself. Large enough for lunch, and dinner, and maybe breakfast tomorrow. The flowers were gone from the wild roses between the willows where he'd made his lair, a hollowed-out spot in a small sandbar near the creek, and he picked a handful of rosehips. A cluster of serviceberry bushes nestled among the willows only feet away, and in moments he had gathered a handful of withered but still sweet fruit.

Soon he had a fire going, a hindquarter of the rabbit was roasting while he munched sour rosehips and sweet berries, and the rest was being smoked. A full stomach would ease his worry about returning to town, losing his temper, and shooting the Marshal and a deputy or two.

Or about how to get into the cave and recover Dolan, or hopefully, Dolan's body.

His paint and the dun were grazing quietly in a small meadow deep with grass now gone brown. He couldn't return to town with the dun horse as he knew Dolan had stolen it when his was killed, and the white eyes would have no respect for the fact he'd recovered the animal, running wild, for anyone to claim. He'd have to take the dun to another town to sell. It carried an Army brand, probably sold as surplus or stolen by whomever its rider had been. Or he could trade it to another Crow for a woman, or firearms, or something of value. It would have to be a very desirable woman to be worth the fifty dollars the dun would bring.

As he tore meat from bone with his teeth, he glanced up and was only mildly surprised to see a man on horseback on the ridge line well over a hundred paces above him, and across the creek on the cave side. The man didn't concern him as he had no weapon in hand that Twodogs could see from this distance.

He shaded his eyes from the sun, and realized it was a young boy, not a man, and he was watching Twodogs eat. When the boy realized he'd been seen, he reined his animal off the ridge line and was quickly out of sight. Twodogs knew of only two white eye cabins on this mountain, the boy must be from one of them.

Settling back, he sucked on the leg bone.

***

I cannot see where the snake is, and there is a ledge above me and a dark recess across the cleft, maybe six or eight feet from where I've plastered myself against the damp wall. It has been all I can do not to release my tenuous grip and slide down the cleft to the bottomless pond. More and more, as I've climbed, the surface is covered with smelly slime; bat guano, I figure.

The snake rattles again, but no more than my backbone is rattling, quivering. A snake bite will sure as hell finish me.

I study the remaining twenty or so feet to the opening above and try to conjure where a snake would have fallen if it wiggled its way too close to the edge? It had to be the ledge just above me...damn the luck. There was no going on without clearing the snake out of the way.

I loosen the heavy bridle from around my arm and let it fall away, grasping the end of the reins, I swing it up so it smacks the surface of the ledge above, and the cave explodes with rattles sending a chill down my back all the way to my exhausted thighs. There must be more than one snake, maybe several.

Maybe a den of vipers.

In the dim light I study the other side of the cleft, but it is not only equally slick with bat crap but even steeper as it nears the bottom. There is no way I can go down and come back up the other side.

I'm afraid to rise up high enough above the edge of the ledge to see what, exactly, I face. Getting hit between the eyes by a big timber rattler would not only likely kill me from the bite, but surely from the fall. At the least, it would blind me.

Carefully I untie the blanket and loosen the rifle.

I have no choice. I have to get the snakes out of my path.

Levering in a cartridge, I ease up far enough that I can extend my arms and get the rifle to fire nearly level across the rock shelf. I pray the snake is not close enough to strike my extended arms.

The report not only nearly dislodges me, but reverberates throughout the cave and the sound disorients and dizzies me. It, combined with the cacophony of rattles, sounds a little like a battle or two I survived in the war…and rattles my backbone nearly as much.

But it seems the rattles are coming from slightly farther away. It seems I've done some good, so I jack in another cartridge and set the cave to vibrating again, then quickly shove and pull myself up high enough that I can see over the edge. Only six feet from me are coiled not one, but three snakes. I get my feet under me enough that I can jack in three shells in a row, and they are close enough I don't even have to sight, and pull off the shots by instinct.

When the echoes of the .44/.40 stop, so has the rattling.

I move on up and onto the ledge and poke the barrel back into the recess where the snakes are now a tangle, and prod them. No movement, so I angle the barrel enough I can drag one my way. Freeing my knife from its sheath, I saw the head off a four foot long timber rattler, then stuff the snake into the sleeve of my coat and jam the rifle in alongside. It will do for more than one meal. Again, tying the blanket across my back, I start up. Another twenty feet, and I will have made it out before dark.

There is no place to sleep other than a narrow ledge, and that would be too dangerous to contemplate.

So, I take a deep calming breath, entreat the good Lord to help me for just a while longer, and begin edging up. This time I use the knife to chip out handholds, for if I don't have them, I'm sure to lose my questionable grip and slide back into the pool.

Far down the mountain, Twodogs jerked upright with the report of a gunshot. He looked up and down the canyon wondering where it had come from, then another rang out and he knew it was across the stream and up the mountain. Somewhere near where he'd seen the boy on the ridge line.

Then three more shots, and he couldn't figure out just where they'd originated. It didn't seem like they came from all the way at the top of the mountain, yet they had a strange muffled sound.

Maybe from all the way over the top.

Probably the boy, hunting. A bad shot if it took five to down a deer or even an elk. Maybe a big griz had risen up in front of the boy...and if so maybe the boy's horse was now free for the picking. Or maybe the boy was eaten but his rifle was still nearby.

One thing he was sure of, the shots weren't aimed at him, so he stood, stretched widely and yawned. Then he packed his few belongings into his blanket, rolled it and tied it to the back of his Indian version of a McClellan, and moved off to saddle his pinto. He would move slowly up the mountain and see what had become of the boy, his horse, and maybe his rifle.

It was worth a few hours.

Revenge of the Damned

Chapter Seven

HELENA WAS A ROUGH AND TUMBLE mining town, a hodgepodge of clapboard, brick, and stone buildings on streets that seemed to have no direction as they were laid out around mining claims. Rough and tumble, but already several miners were millionaires or on their way to becoming. And many were arguing for Helena to become capital of the territory.

Ten years since the discovery of gold in Last Chance Gulch by four old boys from Georgia, who probably either fled the war or were paroled from prison camps if they promised to go west, the city cared little if a woman was killed by her husband for being unfaithful. And the Marshal was among the most respected if not the most respectable citizen and his word was almost sacrosanct. So long as he kept the law, kept the few mine owners from losing their hard-won gold to road agents, and protected those successful businessmen from the Indians, the rowdy cowhands who've begun bringing herds up from as far away as Texas, and from the town's own citizens who wielded the picks and shovels in the mines, he could do little wrong.

And he was well paid for his efforts. Already the town had produced a half dozen millionaires, so the money flowed freely.

Montana had been made a territory in 1864 as a result of so many gold seekers coming first to Grasshopper Gulch, which would become the territorial capital of Bannack, then to Alder Gulch which became Virginia City, and gold was discovered in Helena just a few months after territorial status.

Revenge of the Damned

Now, ten years later, Ulysses S. Grant is president and the country is beginning to come back together after the Civil War; the Transcontinental Railroad is well established; and the country is tied from one side to the other by a wedding of iron rails.

Law is coming to the territory, and even a Marshal has to answer to it.

Judge Homer Stanley sent a missive to Marshal Wentworth:

> *Oscar, we have scheduled a hearing on Wednesday hence in the matter of the death of your wife, Maggie Mae. I would suggest you retain counsel, just to be on the safe side. I might suggest my nephew, Norval Stanley. We'll settle the matter in a morning's time. Then I'd suggest you buy lunch at the Cattlemen's in celebration of your freedom.*

The judge was not a particularly subtle man, having been appointed by Governor James Ashley, and supported by the town's leading citizens. He was known to bend an elbow and never to be one to turn down a bottle of whiskey, a fine loin of beef or elk, or a free lunch.

Wentworth read the message and gave his usual "humph," then turned to the door from his office to the outer room where his two full time deputies kept small desks.

Phinias Portnoy, who was called 'Phil' by most and 'Phony' by many, but only out of his earshot, was out making rounds, but Robert 'Dob' Saltzer was leaning back in his chair reading a month-old Leslie's Weekly. Portnoy was a barrel-chested fella, even larger than Wentworth but far more muscular. He wore a derby hat, carried a belly gun in his pocket and a Remington Army converted to cartridge on his left side. He was right handed, but found it to his advantage to raise his left hand in supplication when faced with a threat—

usually a drunken miner—while he palmed the .32 caliber belly gun in his trouser's pocket with his right hand. He'd been known to shoot a hole in his pants when he thought it was too risky to actually pull the weapon.

Again the Marshal's voice rang out through the doorway. "Dob, get the hell in here."

Grudgingly Saltzer arose and wandered over to lean on the door jamb. "What's up, Marshal?"

"Damn if there's not going to be a hearing on my shooting that damn no good cheatin' wife of mine. Set down here and let's work on your testimony—"

"Hell, Oscar, I didn't see squat."

"The hell you didn't. You want this soft job?"

Dob flushed a little, and nodded.

"Then you saw that little bitch come at me with that compact Remington Double Derringer. Right?"

"You say so, Marshal."

"No, you say so. You know I gave her that little fella for protection and she tried to use it on her loving husband when I confronted her about that...that...that assignation at the Cattlemen's Hotel. I had no choice but to let one fly before she did me in. Right?"

"Yes, sir. I saw her come at you. You had no choice."

"Okay. It's four o'clock. How about I stand you to a beer or two at Sadie's Comfort Parlor. I might even come with a dollar for a token. I hear you are getting partial to some little dove in her place."

Dob grinned wide enough to show his missing canine, knocked out by a miner. "Partial, that ain't the half of it. She's soft as my mare's lips and hot as a mink in mating season. Let's go."

Chapter Eight

THE SHAFT NARROWED ENOUGH that I can get a leg across and I brace myself between the walls. Only ten feet to go.

I edge up, and up, until my head strikes something. I feel up above and realize a tree root has grown out of the wall, and turned to find soil again, leaving a nice handhold around its three-inch diameter. Reaching even higher I find another root, only this one is at least six inches in diameter and its too big around for me grip.

My leg is beginning to quake, trembling from the strain of holding my weight for so long. And it won't last much longer.

Making a decision, I grasped the root I can get ahold of and drop my leg away, and, thank God, I'm able to get a foot hold above the ledge that had held the snakes. I hope there wasn't another quiet one back in the darkness who'll look favorably on a fella's fat calf muscle.

Seven feet to go.

I free my hunting knife and drive it, will all my might, into the fat root above, the one I could not grip. Very carefully I loosen the blanket, and praying I can make the toss, throw the rifle up and out of the opening.

It clears.

Then I do the same with the rattler, and it clears.

I clumsily fold the blanket and try to heave it out, but it opens and floats back, and, luckily, I catch it. Three times I try, then using my teeth and free hand I managed to tie it into a knot larger than my head, and throw it again. This time it, too, is out of the opening, and out of my way.

Getting a foot on another small ledge I push myself up, driving the knife into the wall, and pulling with my arm. It, too, is beginning to shake with exhaustion.

I don't have much time.

Chipping away, I get two more hand-and foot-holds dug. I take a deep calming breath, get one foot in position in a foothold only five feet from the rim with my head and shoulders out. I take the knife in hand and drive it into the surface, and heave, draping my upper body over the rim.

It isn't quite enough, and I began to slip back.

With a Herculean effort, I slam the knife as hard as my worn out shoulder can, driving it deeply into the moist detritus-covered earth.

It holds, and my slide into oblivion has stopped.

I inch myself up and finally get my good leg outstretched, and then a knee beneath me.

"Thank you, Jesus," I say aloud.

With both knees under me, I crawl to a nearby sapling and pull myself to my feet.

Nothing could feel better than my having my feet under me again, as wobbly as they are.

And nothing could feel worse than realizing I'm staring into the eyes of a very large, very ugly, Indian.

"Drop knife," the Indian demands, and the muzzle of the lever action he holds adds emphasis to his command.

And I do so.

"You Dolan?" the Indian asks.

"No, I'm Ulysses S. Grant."

"He chief of the white eye. You no chief. You wounded. You Dolan."

"No, sir. You Sitting Bull or Crazy Horse?"

The big Indian shrugs. "I Twodogs. And wonder if I get more money you alive, or dead."

"Money? I ain't worth a full thunder-pot."

"Made ten dollars tracking you. Ten dollars more I deliver."

"How about twenty if you don't."

The big Indian smiles, which I'm thinking is an event that maybe only happens annually.

"So," I ask, "what's so funny?"

"I kill you, I take all money, then still get ten dollars."

"Lot more than that in that blanket over there," I say, motioning with my head at where the knotted blanket has landed in a mess of buckbrush.

The Indian looks curious and eyes the blanket, fifteen feet from where he stands. Then he motions with the rifle. "You, down."

What the Indian does not see is the rifle, deep in some dried meadow grass, only six feet from where I stand, holding myself up on the sapling.

"Down?" I ask. The longer I stall, the more I'll recover from the climb.

"Down, now," the Indian says, again motioning with the barrel of the lever action.

I take a step nearer the rifle, then let my bad leg collapse under me and fall forward, where I can easily reach the Golden Boy. I groan as I do so, as if I might be unable to get up again.

Twodogs smiles once more, and moves to recover the blanket, his rifle hanging loosely in one hand.

He stops short when the ratcheting sound of my lever action reaches him. To his credit, he doesn't try and recover his own rifle and spin and fire, but merely stops and looks back over his shoulder.

"Where you get rifle? You have no rifle coming out of hole."

"Magic. You want to see it open a big hole in your gut and drain your lunch out onto the ground? That'd be magic too."

"Where you get rifle?" he asks again.

"Ulysses S. Grant gave it to me for killing Indians."

Twodogs says nothing, merely stares, looking as if he's trying to figure out if I really am magic.

"You be real careful now, and put that rifle of yours down on the ground."

Twodogs kneels slowly and places the Winchester in the grass. Then he gives me another tight smile. "You say twenty dollars I no take you to Marshal. Okay."

Now it's my turn to laugh, only mine is a hearty guffaw, then I say, "I need a horse, Mister Twodogs. Where might yours be?"

"Twenty dollars, I sell you one."

"Like you suggested when you had the upper hand, why don't I just shoot your ugly ass and take your horse."

"I hide, you cannot find. Indian hide horse good."

"Okay, Twodogs, tell you what I'm going to do. I don't feel up to hunting all over this mountain for some nag of yours. You give me your horse, I won't shoot you in the knee."

Twodogs stared again, then smiled tightly. "I give you horse you steal in town, keep my horse."

Again, I chuckle. "You give me my own horse back. That ain't no bargain."

"Not your horse. Horse you steal."

"Seems to me Indians think possession is nine tenths of the law—"

"What 'possession'?" Twodogs asks.

"Never mind. We're going to leave your rifle here. You're going to lead me to the horses. I'm going to ride away. I'm not going to shoot you in the knee or anywhere else, if'n you act like a good fella. Then you can come back here and get your rifle. Understand?"

Twodogs nods his head.

I continue, "And if you come tracking me, I ain't gonna shoot you in the knee, but in your ugly head. You understand that?"

Again, Twodogs nods.

"See that loose branch laying over there, the one about my height?"

Nodding again.

"You fetch it up and lean it against that tree there, then move off twenty feet toward the horses."

This time Twodogs nods without being asked if he understands.

He fetches the branch, leans it against the tree, then moves down a game trail several steps.

I limp over to my blanket, recover it, then the branch, which I use as a walking stick, keeping the Golden Boy trained on the Indian. I motion with the barrel of the Golden Boy and we set off down the game trail.

I have to stop a moment, everything's swirling and I'm feeling nauseated. I breathe deeply, let things settle, then follow again.

Now, all I have to do is stay conscious until I get a horse and get away from this crazy red man.

Chapter Nine

JEDIDIAH QUINN SAT HIS GRAY mare a few feet inside a thicket of chokecherry, watching the Indian and the white man a couple of hundred feet down the hill. He'd sat very still for many minutes as the Indian had worked his way up the mountain, praying his horse wouldn't nicker and give away their vantage point.

He'd never seen the Indian before today, but he and his ma had already had their share of Indian trouble since his pa had taken the fever and died...died on Jed's twelfth birthday. It had only been a year, but over the last winter two different bands of Indians had stopped by the cabin and his mama had fed them—not in the house, but giving them a ham out of their smokehouse. A ham they could scarce afford, but as she'd said, they could afford the ham more than they could afford losing their hair and everything they owned.

Jed had a fat young whitetail doe tied across the hindquarters of his mare, and he didn't want to have to run for it and lose the animal. They needed the meat, and two or three more whitetail or an elk if they were going to last the winter.

Their sow had died and they'd butchered the last hog, little more than a shoat, and this doe would join it in the smokehouse, where the sowbelly, small hams, and sausage were smoking. That meat, a hundred pounds of dried beans,

Revenge of the Damned

and an equal amount of flour would last them if the redmen didn't come calling more than once or twice, hungry and demanding.

He should be reining around and beating a trail back up the mountain to the cabin, but what was going on below fascinated him. The man had crawled out of the cave, a cave he knew well although he'd never ventured inside. Never ventured inside because the hole was too dang steep for a man to traverse. The man was covered in what looked to be dried blood, and was obviously gimpy as if wounded. The Indian had threatened the man with his rifle. Jed had considered taking aim at the Injun, only a couple or three hundred feet away, but what if he missed? And what if the Indian, who was half dressed in white man's clothes, wasn't a wild Indian after all? The fact was, there was a band of Indians, Assiniboine Sioux, he thought he remembered, who camped outside of Helena oft times.

And he knew more than one of them had worked for the town, meat hunting, and even tracking for the Marshal from time to time.

What if that Indian was doing honest work? He doubted it, but what if?

So he decided he'd hoist the doe into the crotch of a tree, as high up as he could stow her, and follow along. And keep watch.

Stowing the doe, hopefully, out of reach of wolves and coyotes—hopefully no bear would wander along—he gigged his little mare down the trail. After a hundred yards he could see the two men walking down the trail. Or in the case of the white man, stumbling.

After another forty or so paces they moved out of a small alder grove into a meadow, where two horses were staked and grazing.

But the white man didn't quite make it. He stumbled, fell, tried to get up again, and fell again. The second time he pitched right onto his face, and lay unmoving.

The Indian, almost casually, turned and started back to the white man, whose rifle lay beside him.

Jed reacted without thinking, he raised his little .32 single shot Remington rolling block and fired, kicking up dirt at the Indian's feet.

The redman looked up, then bolted for the horses, grabbing a handful of mane and swinging up, bareback, onto the pinto. He gave heels to the horse and pounded hard to the end of the meadow, disappearing into a stand of massive fir that rose up to the top of the mountain to the south.

Jed quickly fished into his trouser's pocket for another cartridge, dropped the block, and reloaded. He thought about encouraging the Indian's flight by snapping off another shot in his general direction, but he had no ammunition to waste.

Instead, he waited for a good long while, but he couldn't wait too long as the sun was on the horizon and as it was, it would be dark long before he got home. Ma would be worried and ma had had enough trouble.

So he gigged his horse, moved down to within twenty feet of where the man lay, and dismounted. This bedraggled man would not be the first dead man Jed had seen, so he walked right up and kneeled beside him, placing a hand on his chest and feeling for a heartbeat. As still as the man was he was a little surprised to feel a healthy thumping.

He returned to his horse, took the old Army canteen from its spot where its sling looped around his saddle horn, and returned to kneel again.

He poured a little water on the man's face, who shook his head, but didn't open his eyes.

Opening the man's mouth with a firm hand, he poured in a dollop of water. This time the man coughed, rolled to the side, winced and cried out with a deep moan then rolled back with eyes open.

I blink, then wipe my eyes and blink again. "Howdy, young'un," I say, my voice a little weak.

Revenge of the Damned

"Howdy," the boy replies.

"Where'd you come from?" I ask.

"Up the mountain aways. How about you?"

"Bunch of fellas chased me up the mountain from Helena, then some damn Indian—"

"I run the Indian off."

"Good for you, but that Indian may not run far. You best give me another swig of that water then get on home to your ma and pa."

"Got no pa, but I gotta get home to my ma. I'm Jed, by the way."

"You got anything to gnaw on, Jed?" I ask.

"Got some jerky and a chunk of hard tack in my saddle bag."

"I got a paper dollar in my pocket. Would that be a good trade?"

"A dime would be a good trade. 'Sides, I don't want your money. Can you ride?"

"If'n I don't pass out again."

"You keep watch out for that Indian, I'm going to saddle up that dun horse for you."

"Obliged."

After twenty minutes in the saddle the boy had to dismount and tie my legs to the latigo on either side of my dun to keep me in the saddle.

Eventually we got to a meadow, then a cabin and barn. I was stumbling, dazed, and wobbly, and with the help of the boy and a woman got inside the cabin and laid down on a straw filled mattress covered with deer and elk hides in front of a large fireplace.

When the man was settled and sleeping, or passed out, Abby Quinn joined her son Jed at the table while he wolfed down a bowl of venison stew.

She asked, her tone worried, "So, young man, you're now the man of the house, have you brought some fella could be an outlaw into our home?"

Chapter Ten

IT WAS THE FIRST COLD morning of the season, with the trees turning and the cottonwoods beginning to drop some leaves.

Wentworth had been assured by Judge Stanley that the hearing would go as the judge nor any of the men in the room would condone an unfaithful wife. And, certainly not one who pulled a firearm and threatened her husband. Maggie Mae had pretty much kept to herself and had few acquaintances in Helena, and no real friends. She often had begged off even attending the Christian Church, as she was Catholic, although few in town knew it. And, because of the way she was treated by her husband, she seldom left their whitewashed two story out on the edge of town.

When the judge rapped the gavel, and the Masonic Lodge, which was often used as a courtroom, was clearing out, Wentworth approached the table used as the bench and extended his hand.

"Thank you, Homer," Wentworth said, as humble as the judge had ever seen him.

"A real thank you would be supper and a few shots at the Cattlemen's, and maybe sending a couple of prisoners out to cut and stack a few cords of wood. Harmless ones a'course, we want no troublemakers or grudge holders." The judge knocked the dottle out of his pipe, stuffed it, and lit up, then returned his gaze to Wentworth. "Looks to be a cold winter on the way."

"I'll meet you there after I make sure Dob and Phil are making their rounds. Say six?"

He got a nod from the judge.

"How so...the winter I mean?" Wentworth asked, his brow furrowed.

"Why, there's extra fuzz on the caterpillars. Always a sign of a cold winter coming."

"The hell you say. See you in an hour or so."

And another nod came his way.

When Wentworth pushed into the Marshal's office, Dob Saltzer and Phil Portnoy, his two deputies, were hunched on each side of a stool, on chairs, playing cribbage.

"Not disturbing you two fine officers of the law, am I?" Wentworth snapped, twirling his handlebar mustache with one hand as he talked. His deputies knew it was a sure sign of his irritation.

"Damn," Dob said, "I had a twenty crib."

"Fold them up. I got chores for you two."

Dob unfolded his long lanky body and rose, stretching. He walked over beside his little desk and spit a long stream of tobacco juice into the brass spittoon resting there, then swallowed. His prominent Adam's apple bouncing as he did so. Then he turned back to the Marshal, "Phinias here said ol' Stanley said you was justified."

Wentworth narrowed his eyes at the deputy. "And you say?"

Dob laughed, then quickly added, "Hell, Marshal, I'd a shot 'er a few more times, were it some stranger pokin' my lady and her about to shoot me with a belly gun."

Wentworth began to redden, so Dob got serious and shook his head. "Damn if she didn't deserve it. And you sure as hell were justified. But there's some talk around town...."

"What talk?" Wentworth said, raising his voice.

"Just talk, that maybe I was down at Sadie's having a beer when Maggie Mae got shot."

Revenge of the Damned

"You tell anybody mouthing that around to come see me. I'll set 'em straight."

"Yes, sir, I sure will."

"Now, Dob, we still got Crazy Willy McEwen in a cell?"

"Yeah, but he's due to be released in the morning."

"He ain't gonna be. You take him...and...and who else is back there?"

"That big nigra fella, Bama, his workmates on that freight company call him. Short for Alabama, I think."

"What did he do again?"

"He busted the heads of a couple of drummers who were saying the South shoulda won so the likes of him would still be in chains."

"Just knuckles?"

"Yep, that's all the big fella seemed to need. Rosco, the bartender at Paddy's, had to crack him in the head a half dozen times with that big shillelagh he keeps under the bar to get him down. He said the big nigra might have killed the two of them. Even then it took Phil and me and two miners what helped us out to get him in the cell."

"Are the both of them sobered up now?"

"Yes, sir. The nigra's done been quiet as a church mouse and twice as polite since the demon rum wore off. But he done lost his job with them freighters as they done set out for Deer Lodge, and he don't have no horse so he ain't catching up. I know 'cause the freighter come in and paid his wages off."

"Did you collect for the room and board, and if so, where's my seventy five percent."

"In your top desk drawer, like always. We got twenty-five of the twenty-seven dollars he was paid. He weren't real happy, but he just nodded and paid up like a good soldier."

"Not happy?" Wentworth laughed. "That's the way the road apples fall. Tell them both I gave them extra days for being sassy. I want you to take them out to the Judge's place halfway twixt here and the river and put them to chopping wood until the judge has at least three cords put up."

"And I'm supposed to just be a straw boss and keep 'em working."

"Unless you get an urge to pull a crosscut or pick up an ax."

"I can boss."

"That's what I thought. Phil, you got the rounds tonight. I'm buying Stanley supper over at the Cattlemen's."

Portnoy rose and stretched also, then reminded Wentworth, "That big black boy ain't gonna be happy. He's due to be released in the morning like Willy is."

"Tell him he's lucky I don't keep him a year, busting up the heads of two hard working white boys."

"I'll let you tell him."

Wentworth spun on his heel to head to the Cattlemen's, then stopped short. Twodogs, the big Crow, filled the doorway, holding his lever action Winchester in hand, not looking happy and blocking Wentworth's exit.

Chapter Eleven

I AWAKEN HAVING NO IDEA where I am, but I'm warm, and dry, and the smell of baking wafts under the covers I have up over my head. I ease them down just enough to clear my eyes, and can see a woman leaning over a fine cast iron range, feeding a few shards of wood into its firebox.

I start to speak, but then think I might startle her, so merely watch. Then I cut my eyes to the squeak of the cabin door opening and light flooding in. At first, blinded, I can't make out who's there and glance around wondering where my Golden Boy might be. But it's nowhere in sight.

Then I see it's the boy, the boy I remembered who'd helped me, his arms laden with wood. The youth marches over to a wood box next to the stove and drops a couple dozen two inch split chunks of firewood there.

"Thank you, Jed," the woman says.

"You're welcome, mama." Then the boy walks over to where I'm resting on a pallet of hides in front of a fire.

"He's awake, mama," the boy says, sounding pleased at the fact.

"Wa…" I start to ask, but it comes out more a croak than a word.

"Water?" the boy surmises, and I nod. The woman picks up a towel and comes my way, wiping her hands as she crosses the little main room of the cabin.

Her long red hair swings as she walks, brushing her lower back, and green eyes focus on mine. The few freckles on her nose and cheeks did not distract from how pretty she is.

She gives me a tight and somewhat wary smile. "I worried we might have to dig in that hard ground for you. But you've got some color back in your cheeks."

The boy arrives with a mug of water, and the woman puts a hand behind my neck and helps me up enough to drink.

"Thanks," I manage.

"Well, you speak the king's English. You got a name, Mister…?"

"Dolan, Lincoln Dolan. Friends, and it seems you are one, call me Linc."

She smiles, and her smile lights up the room. I am already smitten. "And you are?" I ask.

"Mrs. Albert Quinn," she says, quickly.

"Mister Quinn would be out cutting wood?" I ask.

"He's hunting. He's due back…maybe this afternoon, or evening."

I notice the boy gives her a strange look, and know she's lying. Then I recall the boy saying he had no pa. I clear my throat, then offer, in my most sincere tone, "Ma'am, I appreciate you putting me up like this. I certainly mean you no harm, in fact nothing but gratitude, but the boy told me…sometime ago down the mountain…whenever that was…that he had no pa."

She gives the boy a furtive glance, then turns back to me. "Every living being has a pa, it's just that Jed's father, my husband, God rest his soul, died last winter. One never knows…"

"You're right to be careful, ma'am. Mrs. Quinn. I'll be moving along soon as I can get my legs under me."

She gives me a tight smile. "I don't know who shot you full of holes, or why, Mister Dolan, but so long as you act the gentleman, as you seem to be, we'll tend you. Until you, as you say, get your legs under you. Now, I have some fair to

Revenge of the Damned

midlin' broth on the fire. Jed here's a fine hunter and we'll be having venison stew later on. This is spruce grouse broth, if you'd care for some."

"Ma'am, that would be fine as frog's hair."

She laughs, and takes the mug back to the stove and ladles it full of liquid from an iron pot. Then I can't help but smile as she pulls a platter of biscuits, steaming, from the oven. She splits a biscuit and lathers it with butter. Then from a clay crock she dribbles some honey on the biscuit and heads my way with a plate loaded with a crockery mug and biscuit the size of my palm.

I decided right then, watching Mrs. Quinn work, then cross the room with a platter of food, that I'm in no hurry to get my legs.

Warm, my belly full, I sleep again, only waking when she shakes me.

"Can you sit up enough to eat?" she asks.

"Yes, ma'am. You got a privy outside, I'd guess."

"Of course, but I also have a chamber pot. I need to use the facility myself. While I'm out, please use the chamber pot. Jed will empty it for you."

"Ma'am, I'm not used to being tended—"

"I don't want you out in the cold. And I don't want those wounds to open up. We tended my husband for two months. Jed and I know nursing...in fact I was a nurse down on the Mississippi, and tended many a young man. So, please, just do as I ask."

I can feel my face flush, and nod. She leaves the cabin and I'm able to pass some water. Jed takes the pot and leaves the cabin, and alone, I take a moment to study the place. It's well built, two rooms with a loft over what must be a bedroom. It is well chinked and the fireplace is built from some of the many flat stones I've noticed on the mountain. Mister Quinn was something of a craftsman, I surmise. One window has four small panes of glass, and is shuttered; the second window is merely shuttered, but framed in to receive glass. Glass is expensive, so I figure they'll fill the second when the money's there. I managed to stay upright, leaning against the wall, until she and the boy return.

"Your man was a fine hand with ax and a trowel and mortar."

"He was a carpenter for some time back in Illinois before the war. He found a lime deposit on the other side of the mountain and made his own mortar. He worked hard, and it wasn't fair he…." She seemed to choke up and I'm sorry I've said anything.

But I figure I must continue. "He did right by you and the boy. This is a fine cabin. And you've finished it off fine as a city house." I've noticed two of the chairs have upholstered seats, the table a cloth trimmed with lace or tatting, and there are two samplers on the walls, both white cloth with red crocheting. One proclaiming *Home Sweet Home*, and one *Jesus Is Lord*, next to a small looked-to-be-hand-carved crucifix.

"Thank you," she says, glancing around. "It's simple, but home. We've tried hard to make a home." Then she glances over at the boy, who's perched over the wood box, whittling. "Jed, it's time for your studies."

"Yes'um," the boy says, and crosses the room to a small book case behind a wooden rocking chair. He fetches a book.

"Bible first, then you can go back to Edwin Drood."

"Edwin Drood?" I ask.

"Yes," she says, "*The Mystery of Edwin Drood*, by Mister Charles Dickens."

"I read a Dickens' book, in a trench with grape shot whistling overhead."

"I hope you enjoyed it?" she says, a sly smile on her face.

"*A Tale of Two Cities*, it was the best of times, it was the worst of times. I wish I still had it, as I didn't finish, but it got left in the mud of a trench when we were overrun. Too damn…pardon me, too dang heavy to tote around a battlefield none-the-less." I lay back flat as I'm getting dizzy again.

Then, when my head quits swimming, I offer, "Young Jed is a smart boy, and capable. He saved my bacon."

"He's the man of the house now," she says, and I can see I'd made her maudlin again, and regret it.

"I wish I was up to chores as I'd hunt up some meat or fix a fence, or whatever."

"You will be, Mister Dolan. I'm a fine nurse and I'll have you fit as a fiddle by the new year."

I'm quiet for a moment, then almost choke up, and say, "You plan to keep me in your hair till then?"

"It wouldn't be Christian to heave you out into a Montana winter when you can barely stand, Mister Dolan. You continue your gentlemanly ways, you'll have a warm hearth until you're well."

"There could be some angry folks come hunting me."

"If you're up to telling me about that, it might sooth my soul?"

"Then you deserve to know. Maybe after the boy is tucked away."

Chapter Twelve

PHIL WAS NOT UNHAPPY TO BE left out of the posse that Wentworth formed at dawn. He sat on the porch in front of the Marshal's office sipping a coffee which, unknown to the Marshal, he'd laced with a dollop of Black Widow whisky.

The Marshal reined over and glared at his deputy, "Judge Stanley don't take his coffee till the sun's over the roof top. You work them boys outta earshot till then."

"Yes sir," Phil said and raised his cup to the Marshal and Dob, who reined away followed by Twodogs, and four others who'd just been sworn in.

Twodogs gigged his paint up alongside Wentworth, who turned and snapped, "You ride in the back, dog man till we get back up to that cave."

Twodogs smiled inwardly, knowing where he was going was faster if they traveled up another canyon, but the harder and farther they rode, the less he'd have to listen to the fat Marshal crow. The fat man tired quickly and quieted when he did. Twodogs had another plan, and it didn't include collecting ten dollars from the Marshal. The man they hunted, Dolan, was likely dead of his wounds, but if not, the red man didn't plan to see him die. He'd been impressed when he returned and found his rifle where they'd left it. Dolan knew a man wouldn't last long in the wild without a rifle, and could have easily taken it, but didn't, he was a man of his word, unlike the fat Marshal.

Twodogs settled back in the saddle, knowing it would be three hours to the cave then two more to the first of the cabins he wanted to check.

***

PHINIAS KEPT THE TWO prisoners in leg irons and made them walk in front of his horse the mile and a half to the copse of fir which grew only a hundred yards from the judge's whitewashed, picket fenced, two story. The men carried two double bladed axes, a crosscut, two wedges, and a sledge.

When Phinias finally reined up near a standing dead fir and dismounted, Willy dropped to his butt and began rubbing his chaffed and bleeding ankles,"You gonna take these god dang irons offen us, Phinias?"

"Hell no. Leg irons don't keep y'all from swinging an ax. Y'all get after that fir."

"Ain't gonna do it," Willy mumbled.

"What the hell did you say?" Phinias snapped.

"That fir is eighteen inches through, and sixty feet tall. We ain't no lumber Jacks, and if'n that tree falls wrong while we're all chained up and can't run we're dead men. Ain't gonna do it with no chains on."

Phinias scratched his head, looking up at the tall tree, then laughed. "Hell, Willy, I don't think you could get clear even with them chains off." He reached in a pocket and threw the key to Willy, who knelt and unlocked his restraints.

"You run, Willy, and I'll shoot you like a worthless old dog."

Willy moved to the black man but was stopped short by Phinias, "Not him."

"He can't run outta the way with them chains."

"No loss. Now, get to work."

Alabama stepped back a few feet to study the big fir.

"Where the hell you going?" Phinias snapped.

"Jus' seein' where she gonna fall," Bama said then moved back to the tree and picked up the ax and sunk his first blow two inches into the tree, then instructed Willy, "We gonna put her right across that dead fall and she'll be up off'n the ground and easier to crosscut."

"You fell timber before?" Willy asked.

"Eighty acres worth, then done digged and burned stumps so my daddy had a field to farm."

Willy laughed. "It's your hide she falls wrong."

They chopped until Bama stopped and pointed to a distant spot. "Y'all better take the horse and move on back. Couple more whacks and down she come."

"Thought you knew," Willy challenged, "where she'd fall."

"God knows, all I can do is guess."

Willy and Phinias led the horse out of harm's way and Bama took only three more whacks with the big broad axe. The fir wavered and fell exactly where Bama had predicted.

He got no praise from either Phinias nor Willy.

They went to work trimming branches and then went at it with the crosscut. Then splitting with sledge and wedges. It was three hours before they had a cord stacked.

It was after mid-morning, near noon, when the judge wandered out from his two-story whitewashed house, still in his robe, nightshirt, and slip-on shoes, and walked the hundred yards to where the men worked.

Phinias removed his hat as the judge approached.

"Too long," the judge growled.

"Pardon," Phinias said.

"Two feet is too long. Trim that firewood back to eighteen inches."

"Damn, judge. Why don't we just cut some new to the right length?" Phinias asked, scratching his head.

"Waste of good wood. Trim them back."

Phinias merely shrugged.

The judge walked a little closer to the two, then spoke to Bama, "I thought I only gave you two days?"

Phinias spoke before Bama could reply. "He done sassed the Marshal, who gave him a couple more."

"Marshal's call, I guess," the judge said. With that he turned and headed back.

As soon as the judge got out of earshot, Willy groaned to Phinias, "It's gonna take us hours to saw them shorter. We got no saw horses..."

"Don't matter. Get to cuttin'."

"Phinias, you damn fool—"

"You know, Willy, I always wondered why they call you Crazy Willy. You mouthing off to me. Me with this here Winchester and can shoot you down for flappin' your lip. That's crazy as hell. Get your dumb ass to cuttin'."

Willy clamped his jaw and went to join Bama who'd already found a couple of level limbs protruding from a deadfall that they could use for saw horses, and had trimmed some other dead limbs away to give them room to work. He quickly had a piece of firewood in place to trim.

Phinias walked to his horse and pulled a bottle from the saddle bag, popped the cork, and took a long draw. By the time Bama and Willy were a quarter way through the pile, Phinias had found a nearby standing fir to plop down in front of and lean against. He kept pulling on the bottle while his two prisoners worked.

After they'd trimmed and stacked a half cord, the deputy's head sagged to his chest, the bottle slipped from his hand, and he was snoring, chin on chest.

Willy turned and studied the sleeping deputy for a moment, then walked to where he'd rested the big double bladed axe he'd used and bent down and hefted it.

Chapter Thirteen

"WILLY," BAMA SAID, watching a little wide eyed, "what you doin'?"

Willy didn't answer, just creeped closer to the sleeping deputy. Then with only one hand he swung the axe, a full turn behind him, and brought it down skull center, splitting Phinias's broad-brimmed hat, and his skull, damn near down to the neck.

"Oh, God! Sweet Jesus!" Bama shouted. Then he yelled toward the house, "Judge, Judge!"

"Shut up, you dumb darkie," Willy yelled at him, then bent and pulled Phinias's sidearm, a Remington Army converted from cap and ball to cartridge, from its holster. Then he freed the axe from the man's skull and wiped the blood and gray matter from it on the dead man's trousers. The dead deputy remained leaning against the tree while blood and gray matter dripped off his chin and covered his chest.

Bama went stone quiet and backed away to a large fir, then stepped behind it. Then he snapped his head toward the house with the sound of a door slamming.

The judge stood on his porch, shading his eyes with one hand, a steaming mug in the other. Then he turned and hurried back inside, but quickly reappeared with a small revolver in hand and began striding toward the work site.

Revenge of the Damned

"Keep your mouth shut, darkie," Willy said, standing with the axe in one hand and the six gun in the other, hidden behind a leg.

When the judge got within twenty strides, he again shaded his eyes with a hand, and his face flushed white. "Good God, what happened here?" he asked, looking from Willy to Bama and back again.

"Accident," Willy said, a stupid grin on his face. "Dumb som'bitch done hit his'sef' in the head."

The judge moved a few feet closer. "Who did this?" he snapped.

"He don't know how to use a damned axe," Willy said, the dumb grin still wide.

"That was no accident," the judge said, glaring at Willy.

Then the judge raised the sixgun, but was no faster than Willy, and the guns fired bucking in their hands almost as one. Both men reeled back, the judge going to his back, both hands over a blossoming hole in his chest, Willy collapsing to a sitting position. He dropped the Remington and braced himself with one hand on the ground behind him while the other hand covered a small gushing hole dead center in his chest. He stared down, then glanced over Bama's way.

"The som'bitch done killed me," Willy said, then his eyes rolled up in his head and his body fell backwards, unmoving, eyes open.

Bama could barely catch his breath, but he ran over and picked up the Remington and felt for a pulse in Willy's neck. He shook his head, and began saying the Lord's prayer, which he continued as he moved over to the judge. He felt for a pulse in the judge's neck, and again shook his head, then he looked up and to his great surprise was staring at an older woman. She had flour covering her hands and the blue apron she wore.

"What have you done," she stammered.

"Ma'am, it weren't me," Bama said, and rose, a firearm in each hand.

The woman screamed and spun on her heel, holding her ankle length gingham skirt up, she ran for the house.

"Oh, sweet Jesus," Bama said, looking from one dead man to the other. He moved as quickly as he could, shuffling, to the dead deputy and rolled him over to a prone position and dug in his trousers' pockets until he came up with the large key, unlocked his ankle chains and flung the key and chains aside. He sat for a moment, rubbing his bleeding ankles, then stood, ignoring the pain.

He hurried over, shoved the Remington into a saddlebag and the judge's little Sheriff's Model Colt into his belt. A fine Winchester rifle was shoved into a saddle boot. He tightened the cinch on the deputy's dun, mounted, and turned the animal toward the mountains to the west.

Chapter Fourteen

AFTER SLEEPING THE MORNING away I'm able to sit up and am glad I do as Abbie glances over and smiles with a warmth that would cure the pox.

"Those nice blue Irish eyes of yours are clear and bright, Mister Dolan. That's a very good sign."

"It's your nursing, ma'am. And please call me Linc, if you would be so kind."

"Then Linc it is, and you may call me Abby."

"Short for Abigale, I presume."

"You presume correctly. The boy is Jed, short of course for Jedidiah."

"Son of Solomon and Bathsheba," I say, feeling a little sheepish.

"You know your Bible, Linc," she says, giving me an admiring look.

"Had a pair of folks who pounded it into me," I say, with a smile.

"Did any of it take?" This time she seems truly inquisitive.

"Yes, ma'ma, particularly 'as ye sew so shall ye reap,' and 'eye for eye'."

Her look hardens. "Is that why you got shot up…the eye for eye part?"

I'm sure my eyes harden as well. "Not really, but it might do for those who did the shootin', and who killed a nice woman who believed in the 'do unto others' part."

"Your wife?" Abby asks, again looking very interested.

"No, ma'am. At one time my intended, until the man who became Marshal of Helena lied to her and told her I was blown to pieces in the war. He was my commanding officer, and a proven liar and scoundrel even then."

Abby nods her head thoughtfully, then smiles and asks, "I'm about to have a bowl of stew and a biscuit. Are you up to eating?"

That brings me a wide grin. "Ma'am, you bake as fine a biscuit as any lady to ever grace this good earth. So, yes, ma'am, I'm ready and willin—"

Before I can finish, Jed busts into the cabin, panting heavily.

"What, Jed?" Abby asks.

"Riders. A half dozen. I was trying for a big bull elk which I saw off down the mountain, and didn't see 'em 'til they were only three hundred yards down our trail. They'll be here in a few minutes. That damn big ugly Indian is leading them.'"

"Watch your mouth, Jedidiah," Abby snaps. "You're not so old I can't take the lye soap to your tongue."

"Yes, ma'am, but they're a coming."

I throw the elk pelt down and swing my feet to the floor, then gasp for a moment.

"You can't leave," Abby admonishes.

"I have to, I can't bring this down on you and Jed."

"That, sir, is our choice." Abby moves to a large pie safe against the back wall, where the cabin is dug into the mountain, and pushes it away.

"A cave?" I ask, a little surprised.

"Root cellar, Alex dug it. Get in, quickly."

Jed comes to my side and helps me up, and, leaning on the boy, I hobble to the opening, then turn back to Abby. "You sure about this?"

"Certain sure."

"Where's my Golden Boy?"

"Jed, fetch it. It's under my bed." The boy hurries into the adjoining room and returns quickly with the rifle.

Revenge of the Damned

I disappear inside the dark opening, and Abby and Jed push the pie safe back into place. The cave is not quite high enough for me to stand upright, and only six feet wide, made even more narrow by shelving.

Only tiny shards of dim light enter the root cellar, which is lined on its sides with sawn wood shelves, holding a few canning jars, and bare rocky soil is the back wall as if her man had intended to dig the cellar deeper at some future time. I scoot the eight or so feet to the back wall, lean against it with my legs outstretched, and wait.

I don't have to wait long. Even as deep in the hole as I am, I hear Wentworth's gruff voice from outside the cabin. "Inside the shack, if you're harboring that scum killer, you best send him out before I burn you down."

"Stay quiet, Jed," I hear Abby say, then the sound of the door opening. "What's the meaning of this?" she stammers. "What killer? Is there a killer on the loose?" Abby sounds surprised and concerned. Her voice rises to an octave that Jenny Lind would have trouble reaching. I decide right then that Mrs. Abby may have missed her calling... she's a fine actress.

"You're the Quinn woman," Wentworth snaps.

"I am Missus Quinn, and you sir, should watch your tone when addressing a lady."

Wentworth is silent a moment, then his voice rings louder. "Dob, you and the Crow take a look inside."

"My son's in there. You harm him and you'll rue the day...."

"No one means harm to your son, Mrs. Quinn. We won't be but a moment."

I can hear one booted man enter, and the slight shuffling of another, probably the Indian, wearing moccasins. I carefully check the chamber of the Golden Boy, and feeling a cartridge in place, cock quietly and level it dead center on the back of the pie safe.

And I'm glad I do, as it slides open, but just a foot. I raise the rifle to my shoulder, heat flooding my chest as I know I'm about to be measured for a pine box…but as Abby and the boy are just outside, I'm not about to fire, no matter my fate.

I hear Abby gasp as if she is frightened for her life.

The big Indian leans in far enough to see me at the back of the cave, but to my surprise, raises a finger to his lips indicating for me to stay silent. Then his face disappears and the pie safe returns to sealing the opening.

I can hear the booted man returning down the stairs from the loft, then he yells, "Nobody upstairs."

"No man down," the Indian lies. More footsteps and shuffling, then the sound of the cabin door shutting.

I un-cock the Golden Boy then reach up and scratch my head, wondering what the hell that was all about. The Indian being paid to hunt me and likely due a ten-dollar gold piece if successful, gave me a 'shush' and lied to the Marshal. Damn, if that wasn't confusing.

Everything in the cabin is quiet for a while, then the pie safe swings aside again, and Abby peers in, "You are there. I thought you must have dug in and covered up."

"I'm here," I say, shaking my head, "but don't know why I'm not hanging from one of those high limbs on a ponderosa out across the meadow. This is the second time in as many days I've been saved by a cave."

"How could he miss you?" she asks.

"He didn't, he shushed me and lied."

"You must be big medicine with the Indians," she says, and this time it's Abby shaking her head. "Come on out of there. They're on down the trail hunting you somewhere else. Pshaw, now I've got to reheat the stew."

"Good, I'll need a while for my stomach to settle. Where's Jed?"

"He's mounted up on his mare, following that posse to make sure they're long gone."

I'm quiet for a long moment while she busies herself getting the stew back on the Buck Stove. Then I finally speak, "Abby, I can't begin to thank you and Jed."

"You can thank us by getting back under that elk skin. You cavorting about in your long johns is embarrassing." Then she laughs.

I feel my face flush, realizing that I'm barely decent with nothing between me and total indecency but a well worn red union suit with a saggy flap in the back and a fly about to bust its buttons. I hurry back to the pallet and flop down, pulling an elk hide over myself, then as an afterthought, ask, "Weren't they curious about this pallet?"

"Jed was smart enough to recognize the problem, and whipped off his brogans and jumped under the covers. I guess they thought he'd taken ill and to be truthful, avoided that pallet like it had the pox. I think that was one reason they hurried off like they did."

"He's a fine young man," I say, then repeat, "a fine young man."

I barely get it out before I'm nodding off.

Damn near getting hung will tire a fella.

Chapter Fifteen

THE DUN WAS TOUGH, carrying Alabama up the mountain, not taking a blow until they'd climbed three thousand feet at a steady walk, dodging boulders and thickets, pushing through game trails, crossing creeks.

Finally, nearing sundown, Bama dismounted and led the animal until they came upon a clearing deep in the golden grasses of fall. As the big man had no bedroll, and only the lead rope to stake the horse, he searched the saddlebags for the first time. A box of cartridges for the converted Remington, a sausage—which brought a smile to him—a steel and flint for making a fire, and a picket pin. The last two items made him not only smile, but grin.

He unsaddled the dun, led him to a trickle of water and let him drink his fill, then staked him in the grass. The saddle blanket was wet from the hard working animal's lather, but was better than nothing as a cover—even though unfolded it only stretched from neck to knee.

Before allowing himself to fall asleep, under the cover of a thick chokecherry forty paces from the horse, Bama listened carefully for a long while. Hearing only the sounds of the oncoming night, he finally closed his eyes.

Twodogs had ridden along with the posse, leading them to the other cabin he knew of on the mountain, but they found it vacant, although there was fresh cut meadow grass in a lean-to next to the corral, and signs of day old horse dung in the corral.

The stone fireplace had been used, but was cold to the touch. Whoever had been using the place was gone.

Wentworth began to grumble when they didn't find Dolan at this second location, talking loud enough that Twodogs could hear his insults. He smiled inwardly, glad he'd let the man, Dolan, go undiscovered. When Twodogs had led the man to his horse earlier, and Dolan had tipped his hat and told him his rifle was where they'd left it, Twodogs was surprised. The man rode away, leaving him with his horse and alive. A man would die on the mountain without his horse and rifle, and Twodogs had returned to find it as Dolan had said. Dolan was a man of his word, and a tough man, having two bullet holes in his hide. Twodogs had been a little surprised to see him alive, even with the help of the woman and boy.

Wentworth was a cheat and a liar, and had it been Wentworth at the back of that hole in the woman's cabin, he would have shot him between the eyes, then taken his hair. Not that Wentworth had much hair to take.

The more he thought of the fact Wentworth had cheated him out of the ten-dollar gold piece, the more angry Twodogs became. Finally, as they were riding down the mountain toward Helena, the big Indian gigged his paint up beside the Marshal.

"Want my ten dollars, now." His tone was demanding, but the Marshal was less than impressed.

Wentworth looked over at Twodogs for a long moment before he replied, "Look, Nodogs, I ain't gonna pay you no ten dollar gold piece, in fact I may charge you for not finding Dolan. You're supposed to be a tracker. I don't think your dumb ass could track a buffalo herd through the snow. Now get the hell back and eat our dust while we ride home without the prisoner you shoulda found."

Twodogs glared at him, and dropped a hand to the rifle in his elk skin saddle boot. "My gold piece, now."

"Dob," Wentworth yelled over his shoulder. His deputy had been riding close behind on his dappled gray, and listening to the exchange. Then he turned his attention back to the Indian. "You jerk that damn rifle and I'll beat you to death with it," Wentworth growled, but looked a little on the worried side.

Dob Saltzer, gave heels to his horse and as he passed Twodogs on the side away from the Marshal, swung his Winchester hard, and cracked the Indian across the back of the head who pitched forward and fell from the saddle. Dob reined around and ran over the prostate Indian, unconscious on the ground. The dun horse tried to avoid stepping on the red man, but kicked him in the ribs as he crossed over him, then Dob pulled on the reins, and, backing, his horse stepped on Twodogs.

Dob laughed, and Wentworth cackled. Wentworth yelled at his deputy. "Damn fine job, Dob. Gather up that paint. I'll bet I can get a double eagle for him in town and a few dollars for that rifle."

And even though a couple of the other fellows in the posse complained, they rode away, leaving Twodogs unconscious in the dirt.

Anthony Fellows, the town barber and a deputized citizen who felt he was doing his civic duty by joining the posse, rode up beside the Marshal as they'd moved a couple of hundred yards down the trail. "You just gonna leave him there for the wolves and bears," he said, sounding disgusted.

Wentworth glanced over, and chuckled. "He's a goddamn Indian, or didn't you notice, Tony?"

"He was working for you and the town."

"He didn't get the job done, so we don't owe him road apples."

"Still and all, he could get et, unconscious and all, in the night, and it's damn nigh night."

"At least you got that right. Let's push this up to a cantor. I need a shot of Who Hit John to wash this damn dust out of my throat." Wentworth gigged his horse into a cantor, pulling away from Fellows, who reined back, shaking his head.

Revenge of the Damned

"What a son-of-a-bitch," Tony Fellows muttered, but loud enough that Dob heard him.

"Watch your mouth, barber," Dob snapped, and gigged his dun, following closely behind Wentworth.

"Son-of-a-bitches, a pair," Fellows mumbled, but then he too gave heels to his animal to keep up with the posse.

It was another forty minutes, and dead dark, a moonless night, when Wentworth reined up at the hitching rail in front of his office and dismounted. He yelled at his deputy as he headed for his office door, surprised to see a lamp lit and glowing behind his window. "Dob, get the horses over to the livery and give old Rascal here an extra dollop of oats."

Then he pulled open his door to see Evelyn Stanley, the judge's wife, sitting ramrod straight on the edge of a ladder back chair against the wall—the bustle on her dress precluded her from occupying much more—and two of the city's most prominent miners, both now reputed to be millionaires, Howard Polkinghorn and Delbert O'Brien, standing with hats in hand.

"Gentlemen, Evie," Wentworth said, removing his broad-brimmed trail hat. "What brings y'all here?"

Polkinghorn stepped forward. "Damn if it ain't the worst news," he began, then glanced over at Mrs. Stanley, "sorry, ma'am," then back to Wentworth. "Dang if it ain't...Judge Stanley and your deputy, Portnoy...Phinias...done been murdered. And one of your prisoners, that Crazy fella, shot dead...but he don't matter much I don't imagine."

"Murdered?" Wentworth managed.

"Mur...mur...murdered dead," O'Brien said, stuttering as usual.

Wentworth gave him a condescending glance. "That's what murdered means, Delbert. What happened, exactly?"

Chapter Sixteen

BY THE MOON IT WAS likely approaching midnight when Twodogs awoke, his head aching badly, a cut on the back of his head was weeping blood, his ribs throbbed, bruised and sore. He had a blue-bruise the perfect shape of a horse's hoof on the side of one leg. The rotten white-eyes must have ridden their horses over him.

Wentworth, and Dob, the big dumb deputy, and four others. The only one he knew was the barber, Fellows, he thought he'd heard that was the man's name.

They would pay. His horse and rifle were gone, and unlike Dolan had done, they'd left him on the mountain to die. Only by the blessing of the great spirit was he not in the belly of wolves or the great bear the white man called the grizzly. Had any of those critters, even a pack of coyotes, come upon him while he lay unconscious....

He set out at a brisk pace. It would be after midnight when he reached the white man's town, which was perfect. They would all be asleep or drunk. Drunk was the white man's way.

Had he not hurt so badly he would smile. But he would wait, and smile after they were all dead and their hair hung from his coup stick.

Two hours walking briskly, trotting some, mostly downhill, then he slowed to an easy walk as he approached the lights of the town. There was a lamp lit in the lobby of the Cattlemen's Hotel, and all six of the saloons, one at the edge of town, five on Last Chance Gulch, were brightly lit and sounds of miners, drovers, and drummers rang out through batwing doors. Piano playing came from two, and a banjo plinked from a third. Beauregard's Bucket of Blood, Sweet Mary's, and the Cattlemen's he was able to slip up to and study the crowds through panes of glass.

He did not want to be seen, as he was wanting those who'd left him on the trail to think him dead, so he was very careful.

The damn fools had taken his rifle and horse, but had left him with his knife, and it was enough. He'd traded a buffalo hide, nicely tanned by the Crow women, for his knife, and it held an edge as good or better than the flint he'd used as a boy.

It would do nicely for the purpose he had in mind.

He did not see the Marshal or the deputy, Dob, among any of the crowds in the saloons. But he thought he knew where he would find the barber. Lights often glowed at the rear of the barber shop, well into the night. The barber must live behind his place of business.

So he moved into an alley he knew led to the barbershop, which was sandwiched between the large two story Mayberry's Mercantile with rooms rented to miners on its second floor, and one of the town's two liveries.

Knowing he wasn't at his best, with head still pounding and ribs and leg aching badly, but, none-the-less, it was time to avenge what had been done to him.

Just as he approached the small door and adjacent window leading from the back of the barbershop into the alley, a hound lunged from between the mercantile and the barbershop, barking loud enough to awaken any but those sleeping off a quart of whiskey.

He backed away and across the alley to crouch between some crates and waited for the cur to settle down. He did, chased his tail in a circle a couple of times, yawned, and dropped his head to sleep.

Twodogs waited a half hour, not moving, not making a sound, and it was good he did as he heard a door slam, then a light was lit in front of the barbershop and the man they called

Fellows carried a lantern into the room at the rear. Twodogs had been lucky, had he broken in earlier the man wouldn't have been there.

Now, he knew he was. Another half hour passed, the first fifteen minutes or so with the lantern burning in the man's room, the second with it out.

Twodogs slipped across the alley to the door. He listened and was pleased to hear the man snoring loudly. He tried the door, but found it latched.

Slipping the knife from its belt scabbard, he moved a step back, and slammed a moccasined foot into the door. It swung aside with a loud crash.

"What the...," came from a corner of the room, and Twodogs sprang that way, slashing with the knife as he could see nothing but sensed movement. And the edge of the sharp steel caught something, and the barber screamed.

"Jesus, you cut me," he cried out, and Twodogs slashed again, this time higher.

"No, no..." the man screamed again, and Twodogs slashed at the sound.

Twodogs' eyes were adjusting to the extra darkness of the room, and this time he could make out the whites of the man's eyes and he sliced, back and forth, back and forth, now the man didn't yell, but gurgled.

Twodogs stepped back, and the man crashed to the board floor. The Indian moved to the open doorway, and listened. The dog was barking again, but no other sounds...no running footsteps, no yelling men. Nothing.

He reached for the man's hair but there wasn't a handful, so he sawed off an ear and shoved it in his pocket.

The only member of the posse who'd stood up for Twodogs, was dead by his hand.

Now, in the dark and silent room, he took his time. He found a rifle leaning in a corner and a gun belt hung from a chair. Two apples were in a bowl on a small table flanked by two chairs.

He took an apple with him, munching as he went.

He was well armed again, but still afoot. So he moved next door to the livery stable, ignoring the barking dog. Like the barber, he knew the hostler lived where he worked, but his room was upstairs in front of the hay loft, overlooking the street.

The Indian casually moved through a small corral at the rear of the place, then inside from stall to stall, and was pleased to discover his paint. His elk skin saddle was nowhere to be found, so he selected one with a bridle hanging from the horn and a bedroll strapped to its cantle, from a half dozen perched on a rail, and fitted a blanket and it to his paint horse.

He wished he knew where the deputy, Dob, bedded down, but couldn't check every room in Helena without being discovered, and there were dozens in the boarding houses and hotels. And he wished even more he knew where the Marshal lived. Both were unfinished business. But it's better to live to fight again than take unnecessary risks. And he had enough blood on his hands for one night.

They could wait.

He knew where Dolan was, and the man owed him a ten-dollar gold piece, after all, he'd given one up when he didn't turn Dolan over to the Marshal.

So he'd go there, and let the white man's town get back to normal, then he'd return.

Chapter Seventeen

IT WAS NINE THE NEXT morning when Wentworth entered his office. Dob, his deputy, had the coffee brewed and to the Marshal's surprise, his office was filling with townspeople. The mayor, Johnathan P. Dougle, five feet six inches of pure hell-on-wheels, greeted him a little sarcastically, "I guess the low-down murder of a judge and one of your deputies doesn't bother you much, Oscar."

"That four in hand tie a little tight on you, Johnathan? It cuttin' off the blood to your brain...of course it bothers me. I been home composing a telegram to send out. I'm glad you're here. You and the council. I want you to authorize a thousand dollars reward for that nigra son-of-a-bitch, a thousand for Dolan, and another thousand for me to hire some fellas I know from down Bozeman way."

"You need another deputy, with Phinias dead, but Marshal? How come--"

"Yes, sir," Wentworth snapped, poking the mayor in the chest with a fat finger. "I want to hire four hands from Bozeman, if they're still there. Last I heard Joaquin Guzman, the Tollofson brothers, and a fella who was a marksman and rode with Bloody Bill Anderson or Quantrill or some yellow belly som'bitch, were thinking of wintering over down that way. Stanley McCallester I believe is the shooter's name. They just finished a job for General Frank Stoddard, who has substantial cattle ranches in the Paradise Valley along the Madison. Word I got is they killed over twenty of the

Brooksbury gang, hung one every mile, Brooksbury included, from a Cottonwood, along the river as a warning to others. Rustlers all who'd been helping themselves to the General's cattle."

"You need four shooters to run down one nigra?"

"And Lincoln Dolan," Wentworth pressed.

Wentworth glanced from man to man, Delbert O'Brien a miner and city councilman, Howard Polkinghorn also a miner and city councilman, Forrest Mayberry the owner of the local mercantile, Wilfred McAllister was the station master at Huntley's, and Tiny Allendorf who ran the Cattlemen's Saloon and Hotel. They had a quorum and could approve anything Wentworth needed.

"I can't see it," Dougle, the mayor, said scratching his van Dike beard, then glancing from councilman to councilman, who likewise were shaking their heads.

"Too damn much—" Dougle began, but was interrupted when the Marshal's office door flew open and crashed against the wall so hard that dust motes floated from the ceiling.

"What?" Wentworth asked.

Morris O'Shaughnessy, the town blacksmith, filled the doorway. The burly man with a full head of black curly hair and five days of beard stood there panting.

"Fellows," he stammered, "the barber...I went over to get a shave and a trim...and Tony Fellows."

"Get it out, man," Wentworth snapped.

"He's dead. The door was locked and Tony always opens exactly at half past seven. So I banged on the door and got no answer and walked around to the back. Sure enough, the door to his room was kicked in and there he was. Dead as a dog turd and twice as ugly, all cut to hell-and-gone from stem to stern. Blood like a slaughter house, covering the place."

"Let's go," Wentworth said, and started for the door, then stopped so suddenly the mayor ran into the back of the much larger man, dislodging his hat. As he was readjusting it on his almost hairless pate, Wentworth stuck a corn cob size index finger in his chest. "Now, Mister Mayor, you think we need some deputies to help us out a while. We got us a stampede of killers here. They're the damned, and the damned got to be sent packin' straight to hell. Damned to hell."

Johnathan stammered. "Damn if we might not need 'em. We'll bring it up at the council meeting tonight."

Wentworth lowered his voice. "Four dead in two days means we got us a serious problem. Dob here is good to patrol the streets and lock up a drunk, but I need some men can ride and shoot. I'm sending a telegram to Bozeman soon as we see what happened to Fellows."

Johnathan glanced back, and got a nod from the councilmen. Then turned back and looked up at the Marshal. "One month, no more than fifty dollars each. And the rewards are five hundred each. That'll get the attention of some poor pilgrim who'll turn 'em over."

Wentworth shook his head. "Might take a hundred each for the deputies."

"Then a hundred, but no more, and no more than four hired and no more than a month."

"Let's see what's happened to our barber. Who the hell is going to cut my hair," Wentworth mumbled as he strode past O'Shaughnessy.

Chapter Eighteen

WITH THE SUN NOT YET over the low mountains to the east, Bama stood in the dark cluster of chokecherry and watched the man on the paint horse as he eyed the dun Bama had staked out. He knew by the man's hesitant manner that he had evil intent in mind.

The man, who he figured was an Indian due to his long hair to the middle of his back and the feather he wore in his hair, even though he wore white man's trousers and shirt, dismounted and moved stealthily to the dun. He glanced from side to side as he approached.

The big black waited until the Indian reached down and pulled the picket pin, then he moved forward out of the thicket, the Remington Army in his right hand, the Colt Sheriff's Model in his left.

"You like my horse?" Bama asked, a little louder than need be as he was only twenty paces from the man.

Twodogs almost tripped over his own feet as he stumbled away from the dun. He reached for his holstered sidearm, but Bama cocked the Remington, aimed with an outstretched arm, and shook his head and yelled, "Don't."

So Twodogs didn't. He dropped his arms to his side and shrugged. "Loose horse," he said.

"Staked out, hardly loose. You a horse thief?"

"No. But I find horse...."

"You'd let a fella face these mountains without a horse?"

Twodogs was silent for a moment, then said, "Killed fat sage hen. You want share."

Bama lowered his two sixguns. "Sure 'nuf. You got a fire?"

"No. I got flint and steel. You get wood."

"Deal," Bama said, and headed back to the thicket where dried limbs and twigs crisscrossed the ground.

He returned with an armful, but still cautious, held the small Sheriff's Model in one hand. When he saw the Indian had retrieved the sage hen and was plucking away, he dumped the wood near where Twodogs already had a small fire burning.

He brushed off his hands and extended his right. "Alabama, most call me Bama."

"Twodogs," the Indian said, trying to brush the feathers away, then merely nodded and went back to plucking.

"Don't you fellas run with a tribe or some such thing?" Bama asked, as he fed some larger dried limbs to the fire.

"Not big, too much smoke," Twodogs cautioned about the fire. Then added, "Men see."

"You got fellas looking for you?"

Twodogs shrugged.

So Bama continued, "What for? I got fellas a huntin' me, I bet."

"Why for?" Twodogs asked.

"They think I killed a couple of fellas. I didn't, but the law don't believe no black man."

Twodogs gave him a tight grin. "They think I kill a fella, I bet."

"Did you?"

"Needed killin', more need killin', steal my goods, leave me to die."

"Sounds like this fella needed killin'. So, we're in de same boat?" Bama said, returning the tight smile.

"We move together, one sleep, one watch for posse," Twodogs offered.

"Suits me. I ain't looking forward to stretching no rope."

Twodogs nodded, then skewered the hen on a branch and propped it up over the fire with a couple of stones.

"Which way we headed?" Bama asked.

"Up the mountain aways. Snow come soon. White man lazy. I know man who is hunted. He has woman, cabin, barn, food. We go there."

"Will it be safe?" Bama asked.

"More safe than forest in snow. Cabin high on mountain."

"Why don't we just keep on moving?"

Twodogs looked at him like he was loco. "White man have talking wire. All white men know Twodogs wanted. Besides, I have debt to settle with Helena people."

"Well, I don't."

Twodogs laughed out loud this time. "You black man. Big black man. I only see big black men can count on one hand. Wire say watch for big black man. Wanted dead or alive. I hunt you, big black man, for money for dead or alive, I take you dead."

"You got a point, Mister Twodogs."

"Better we hide out where plenty game, plenty water even in winter...I know hot springs, plenty firewood...and maybe we trade with Dolan—"

"Dolan?"

"Other wanted man on mountain. He owe me and he man of honor. Maybe we trade and last winter. Then maybe white man forget Indian and black man, and move on. Many white men die in city before Spring, so white man busy. Must be many tribes…kill each other."

This time it was Bama's turn to shrug. "Good. Then I head back to Fort Benton and get a job on a sidewheeler headed back down river."

"And I kill more white men and go Crow country."

"Ain't no skin off'n my black ass," Bama said, with a shrug.

Twodogs lay back in the grass and closed his eyes, while the bird cooked.

Bama decided since the Indian's horse was saddled, he'd better be as ready to beat a trail, so he headed to where he'd hidden the dun's tack and returned and saddled the gelding. When he'd finished, the Indian was back up. Twodogs pulled the barely cooked bird off the fire.

"Tear him in half. I'm gonna cook mine a bit more," Bama said, and Twodogs shrugged and did so.

But he cautioned, "No waste time. Get higher on mountain. Posse get this far before tire out."

Bama nodded, and decided the bird was done enough, and ripped the red meat from the bones.

He really didn't want to hang, particularly for something he didn't do.

Chapter Nineteen

A CROWD HAD GATHERED outside the barber shop's door, actually the door to the barber's small room opening to the alley. Wentworth, with Dob close behind, elbowed them aside then stopped short when he saw the grisly scene. Blood splattered the walls and pooled on the floor under the man's body. Dressed in a night shirt which was sliced to tatters, he lay with arms and legs askew in unnatural positions.

Wentworth stepped inside then turned and put a hand on Dob's chest, "Keep the sightseers out of here and send someone after the digger."

The Marshal knelt and studied a footprint, clearly delineated in the blood. Immediately he could see the print had no heel, a moccasin. A damned Indian, likely. Twodogs, likely. He'd send a man back up the trail to see if there was any sign of the Indian, or his body, on the trail. But he didn't say anything. He'd get his deputies and his reward money, more likely, if they thought this was the same killer who'd done in the judge, the deputy Phinias, and his prisoner Willy McEwen.

"Damn, if he didn't take his'sef a prize," Wentworth mumbled to himself, noticing that Fellows' ear had been cut off, and didn't appear to be laying about. He rose and walked through a connecting door to the barber shop with its two barber chairs, mirrors, four ladder-back chairs, and a couple of cabinets. He moved to the cabinet behind the chair and closest to the multi-paned window, nearest the street, and bent and pulled aside a cloth covering three shelves. Mugs of soap, razors, a strop, and a small tin box. He picked up and opened the box, then glanced over his shoulder to make sure no one had followed. Then he pocketed the twenty seven dollars Fellows kept there, earnings and change, and walked back in the other room to see that Winiferd Willoby, the undertaker, was in the room bent over Fellows' body, almost losing his black top hat in the process.

"You been busy," Wentworth said, and Willoby glanced up.

"No rest for the wicked," Willoby said, and gave the Marshal a tight serpentine smile.

"I guess you won't have need of the doc to help with a cause of death," Willoby chuckled. "Not unless you think he cut himself shaving."

"How about you get that coffin builder of yours over here to board this place up after I get someone to swamp it out."

"Will do, Marshal. Who's paying?"

Wentworth shrugged. "No money in that nightshirt nor on the premises. If he don't have a bank account we can draw from, the city will cough up. Keep the cost down. Fellows wasn't a wealthy man."

The undertaker nodded, and Wentworth moved out into the crowd. He stopped next to Dob and instructed, "Go to the Cattlemen's and ask Tiny to send a maid over to clean this place up. One with a strong stomach."

"He'll want to know who's paying?"

"The city will come with four bits, and he'll owe me a beer."

"How about he owes us both a beer."

"Just get your ass over there."

"Yes, sir," Dob said, and spun on his heel.

I awaken feeling much stronger, and after a breakfast of flapjacks, side pork, and a couple of cackleberries, am ready to find my way out to the privy.

"You sure you can walk?" Abby asks.

"I got to the table...of course your cooking is a great enticement."

"You want me to help you outside?" she asks.

"Jed can walk along to make sure I don't plow your yard with my nose."

She laughs and motions for her son to get up and go along.

After I'd done my business in the small privy between the house and a long lean-to that serves as barn, attached to a lodgepole-rail fenced corral, I lean on the boy for a moment. Then say, "Stay with me boy, I want to check on the horses."

"Right beside you, Mister Dolan," the boy says, and moves slowly along, between some scratching chickens, as I hobble to a pass-through door, and enter.

I'm surprised to see the small barn, maybe twelve feet by twenty-four, is as tightly built as the cabin. It, too, is backed to the hill, dug in, and it, too, has a cave dug deeper into the hillside, only this one is almost as long as the barn. More to my surprise is a draw-down table for saddle making, a trade I'm fair at, and a half dozen saddle trees in various stages of completion.

A large critter-size door opens into a corral, and the back of the barn has an eight by eight stall that opens outside with a hog-size swinging door. The other four feet of the end is a four by eight foot chicken coup with a high opening and small hinged door only a foot square. And some pole roosts and laying cubicles that can be reached from inside the barn. Only one red hen rests in a hutch cubicle. The hutch, like the floor of the barn, is lined with hay. What I figure must have been the pig pen had at one time been hay covered, but now is not so neat as the rest of the inside. If there had been hogs, they are now missing and the normally pungent odor of fresh pig dung is absent.

"Your pigs out running in the forest?" I ask.

"The sow took a fever and we butchered the last two, only about sixty or seventy pounds each...but mama was afraid to wait as they might sicken as well."

I nod. "Probably wise."

I study the rest of the room, and the end wall flanking the door where we'd entered is neatly lined with tools. Drawing knives, a half dozen saws of various shapes and uses, awls and punches, and other well-kept items. And bins, with square nails and expensive screws, and wooden pegs of various sizes. A one gallon crockery mug is filled with glue, now dried and confining a brush in its stiffened mixture.

"Your daddy was a saddle maker?" I ask the obvious.

"He claimed to be only a fair hand with leather. Mostly he carved and assembled saddle trees. Sold them for a dollar a piece to saddle makers all over the territory. He traded a half dozen for finished saddles a time or two."

"What's this wood he used?" I ask.

"Larch, he liked it because it was easy to work, yet strong and light. Sometimes, if he could find it and needed an extra strong horn he used hickory. He found some wrecked wagons what came from the east and scavenged a fair pile of hickory. He scrapped out one wagon came from Washington...said it was teakwood. Wagon was likely built from ship's ricking that sailed the South Pacific...least that was what pa thought."

I glance over at a small potbelly stove. "He must have worked out here plenty to have a stove."

"All winter long. When we weren't hunting or gathering firewood he was spending his time carving and peggin' and gluin' and putting saddletrees together."

Picking up a nearly finished tree, I roll it around and study the joint work. "He did beautiful work," I say, then notice the boy is tearing up.

I place a hand on the boy's shoulder. "And he raised a fine son, Jed. Now give me a hand so I can get back inside and sleep off that larripin' good breakfast."

"You gonna stay with us?" Jed asks, wiping away a tear.

"Got to stay long enough to work off all your ma's done for me."

Jed nods, and moves along beside me back to the cabin.

Abby is waiting in the doorway, watching to make sure we're getting safely back.

Chapter Twenty

IT WAS LATE AFTERNOON before Bama and Twodogs made it to the Quinn cabin. They sat in the deep shadows of thick lodgepole pine, across the meadow and trickle of a creek that served as pasture for the Quinn's two horses and swayback milk cow. They had killed a cow elk on the way up the mountain, and both horses carried not only the men, but saddlebags full of meat with fore and hindquarters hanging across their rumps.

"What think?" Twodogs asks his new saddle mate.

"Sure'nuf don't know. Don't seem to be a soul about, 'cept they's smoke from the cabin."

"Ride up, I cover," Twodogs suggests. "Ask for Dolan."

"Why not you?" Bama replies.

"Know me. Maybe not welcome."

Bama shrugs, then gigs the dun out of the pines, through the meadow dodging the staked out cow, who eyes him carefully, then stops fifty feet from the cabin door.

"Hello the cabin!" he shouts. Then again, "Howdy inside. Anyone about?"

In the cabin, Abby moves quickly to the pallet and shakes me awake. "We've got company." Then she moves to the pie safe and pulls it away from the wall as I gather up my Henry Golden Boy and rise, but rather than gimp my way to the cave, I make my way to the shuttered window that holds no glass, and peer through the crack.

"One man...man of color. No weapons in his hands."

Jed had been in the loft doing his studies, but now hurries down the stairway, which is nearly as steep as a ladder. "Let me—"

But I interrupt. "Get your rifle, Jed, and talk from the doorway. I've got your back."

"Careful, Jed," Abby cautions.

Jed carefully opens the door, but only six inches. "Howdy," he calls out.

"Need to speak to Mister Dolan," Bama says.

"Nobody named Dolan here," Jed shouts back. "You with the posse?"

Bama was quiet for a moment, then answers, "Ain't no posse with me. Fact is, they got about as much want for me as they got for Mister Dolan. Might I have a talk with him, youngster?"

Jed glances over at me. I nod and limp to the door.

"What can I do for you?" I call through the crack.

"They calls me Bama. I rode up here with Mister Twodogs. Seems he had a bit of a fallin' out with Marshal Wentworth. I had to run from somethin' another body done did, and they are huntin' me and him both. Winter is coming on, and we done thought we might hole up in that there barn."

"The winter?" I reply quickly. "Mrs. Quinn doesn't have provisions for more than she and her son."

"We got us a cow elk to add to the larder, and Mister Twodogs and I will fill the smokehouse, you give us a week."

I glance over at Abby. "You want more company?"

"We can put them up for the night, in the barn, and I'll cook up some of their elk for them. But I'm feeling fortunate that you've proven to be a gentleman. I couldn't be that lucky with two more on the run from the law."

"Y'all can stay the night in the barn, then you'll have used up your welcome. Mrs. Quinn will cook up your supper, but you'll take it in the barn. Agreed?" I open the door wide, so the big black man can see I'm well heeled, with a revolver in my belt and the Golden Boy hanging loosely at my side.

"Well, sur, that be better than sleepin' in the woods with no bedroll and all. Send the boy out when we get settled in and we'll give him a chunk of loin for his ma to cook up."

Twodogs spurs his horse out from the woods, and waves at me like a long lost relative.

I give him a small wave in return, then nod at Bama. "It's getting some frost and is clouding up. There's a stove in the barn and a half dozen saddle blankets out there. Get settled in and a fire going and the boy will be out when Mrs. Quinn is ready for the meat. You sure no one's followin' y'all?"

"We sat on a high spot and watched our back trail and could see all of two miles. No one was a coming. Besides, Mister Twodogs is real clever at leaving no tracks."

"I'll bet he is. Still, the boy will ride back aways and take another gander. I don't want to chance no gun battle hereabouts. Mrs. Quinn has had enough grief."

"No, sir. We'll light a shuck outta here, any sign of trouble on the way."

"Fair enough." I shut the door, and wave Jed over. "You hear that?"

"Yes, sir."

"You okay with all of it?"

"I'll ride back to where I can see a long way down the canyon."

"You stay until you think you can just make it back in the light, understand?"

"Sir."

I turn to Abby. "I don't mean to take liberties with your hospitality, ma'am."

"All's fine. Tomorrow you can head them out of here, fed and rested."

"I'd feel better if I was up to snuff," I say. "We won't let them in the cabin."

"At least not more than one at a time."

"You're the boss. I'm sure it'll be okay," I say, but know I don't sound convinced.

Revenge of the Damned

"I might be able to explain one wanted man away to a posse, but it's looking like I'm harboring a gang."

I smile tightly. "We'll get shed of them tomorrow."

Abby nods, but she doesn't look convinced either.

Marshal Oscar Wentworth was disappointed that it would be a month, or more, before Joaquin Guzman and his gunmen would arrive, as he'd sent word he would continue his hunting until he had an elk, grizzly, buffalo and mountain lion.

And the Marshal was getting pressure from the powers-that-be in the city. He had to do something, and the damn weather was worsening. He would be surprised if it didn't snow this very night.

Hell, he would send Dob and hire a couple of glory seeking cowhands or even town drunks, to try and track down his growing list of murderers. He had absolutely no faith that they would have an iota of success, but doing even that would keep all the smart ass new town millionaires off his back until Guzman arrived.

He had a front-and-center this very evening at the monthly city council meeting, and he had to have a plan, and Dob and the drunks were it...at least for the time being.

Even if the three got their dumb asses shot fulla holes, it was better than doing nothing, and no loss.

One thing was for sure, the Marshal wasn't going on the hunt with the smell of snow in the wind.

Chapter Twenty-One

ABBY WATCHED THE TWO MEN move into the barn and lead their horses into her corral with her mare and Jed's. Obviously, the Indian's paint was a stud and the dun cut proud as they began acting up around the mares. She knew enough about horses to know stabling them together probably wasn't going to end up well...but had more to concern her with the two very large men in close quarters. And both admittedly running from the law.

She turned to me, as I'm back on my pallet, "Link, I fear I made a big error letting those two take shelter in the barn. They're a rough looking pair...that black gentleman is big as two men and looks ox strong. The Indian has savage written all over him. What are we going to do?"

I smile at her. "Other than the privy, you won't have to get near them."

"I do believe it will be the privacy of my room and the chamber pot for me until they have departed."

It is only an hour, and Jed has returned. Before she sends him out to pick up the meat they'd promised she gives her son an admonition to be careful.

"Yes, ma'am," he says. "Shall I take my rifle?"

I interrupt, "Jed, let's show good faith until they prove not worthy of it. Don't take your rifle, take a smile and a glad hand. They could have lain in wait outside and shot you or me down, if they had evil intent."

"Yes, sir. A smile."

"And a hand offered in friendship, until the other fella proves otherwise."

Jed nods and makes his way out the door. Abby, apprehensive, watches thru the crack in the shutters until Jed enters the barn.

"What?" I ask.

"Nothing, just being an old worry wart."

"Prettiest wart I ever saw," I say with a smile. "If you don't mind my saying so."

She laughs. "I'm not exactly sure that's a compliment, but I choose to take it as one."

"And it was meant as one."

"Then, thank you, sir." She turns back to the crack. "He's coming back with half an elk loin. We're going to have a feast tonight."

Jed hurries into the cabin and drops the eighteen inches of elk loin, the large end as big as my bicep, on the table, then asks, "Ma, Mister Bama said he'd teach me to play cribbage. He saw pa's deck of cards out there and is using pa's drill to make a board. May I go back?"

She glances over at me, "Linc?"

"Don't sound like evil intent to me," I reply and give her an encouraging smile.

She instructs him, with her brow furrowed. "Go, but a half hour you be back here and bring in an armful of wood when you do."

"Yes, ma'am. I got a snowflake on my nose on the way back. We may have a layer of white come morning."

"Then make it a big armful of wood."

"Yes, ma'am," he says, spinning on his heel.

"Linc, you get some rest," she instructs me like a schoolmarm. "I'm going to grab some potatoes and dried or canned fruit out of the cellar and what would you think of a peach cobbler?"

"I won't be able to sleep, just thinkin' on it," I say, and laugh, but lay my head back and close my eyes.

Wentworth had a coffee cup laced with Who Hit John in hand when Dob returned from making his afternoon rounds. Oscar could see Dob was in his cups, probably stopping at every saloon in the gulch to mooch a free drink and gab with the pleasure ladies. He was slurring his words.

"Nothing going on to complain about," Dob said, plopping into a seat across the desk from the Marshal.

"You're drunk," Oscar accused.

"Had two beers at the insistence of the owners, Oscar. You said to keep up good relations with the folks."

"You call me Marshal Wentworth during work time, damn it. And it's work time damn near all the time, unless we're fishing or bird huntin'. Got it?"

"I got it, Marshal Wentworth." But his tone was sarcastic.

"You ain't drinking no more tonight."

"Hell with that, Oscar...Marshal I mean. I'm off work in fifteen minutes and I promised—"

"Don't give a damn who you promised. You got to get out there and hire a couple of old boys to ride out with you tomorrow morning...early."

"What the hell for?"

"You're going hunting."

"What the hell for?"

"A big black and that damned Dolan, that's what for."

"Jesus, Os—Marshal. It's liable to snow. It's sprinkling cold rain out there right now."

"Then I guess you better break out your slicker. Get out there, get somebody on the payroll."

"Who the hell am I gonna hire to ride out in this weather?"

"Two dollars a day each. I don't give a damn who, so long as they got a firearm and a decent horse. Hell, I don't even care if they have a horse. You can hire them a horse. And hire a pack mule and stock up at the Mercantile before Mayberry closes."

"How the hell long am I gonna be out in the wild?"

"Three or four days, just to keep the city fathers off'n my back."

Dob shook his head in disgust. "I gotta ride in the damn weather just so you can look like you're doing something?"

"Either that," Wentworth snapped, his voice raised, "or ride the hell out of Helena after drawing your pay. What's it gonna be?"

Dob clamped his jaw, then mumbled, "I'll go see who's up for a hunt."

"Thought so."

Chapter Twenty Two

ABBY ROASTED THE LOIN, whole, in the fireplace, fried up a half dozen fat potatoes and a couple of fist sized onions in a cast iron fry pan, and sent half the loin, spuds, and onions out to the barn in a milk pail along with a quart canning jar from which she'd removed the peaches and filled with buttermilk.

She instructed Jed that he'd have to wash the pail after they were finished, and milk Bessie the cow, after he'd eaten his share of the steak and vegetables with us in the cabin.

After dinner she sent the boy out with a plate full of peach cobbler and instructions to return with the milk. She was surprised when he quickly returned with the half full pail.

"That's the fastest—" she began.

He laughed and says, "Mister Bama already milked old Bessie into a crock and fed the horses a forkful of grass each. I like having them fellas around."

"Don't get too used to it," Abby says, and sits with her cobbler to join Jed and me.

As they prepare for bed, the wind begins to howl. Abby peeks out the door and turns to me. "Old man winter is paying us his first visit. The snow is blowing flat level and our guests have brought the horses and the cow inside the barn."

"Well, that saves us having to do it."

"It does," she says, her voice softening. "How am I going to throw them out come morning?"

"It'll melt off come the first sun. Maybe not tomorrow but for sure the next day."

"Maybe," she says, "maybe not."

And it was maybe not tomorrow, as morning came with a full foot of snow on the ground and still softly falling. The wind had quieted, but the sky was still dark and ominous.

Abby cooks up a hash with leftover potatoes and steak and sends Jed out with servings for each of the men in the barn, when he returns he informs her, "Mister Bama said to thank you and to ask you when you wanted them to pack up and light out?"

Abby slumped back in her chair, then glanced over at me as I'm finishing my coffee. "Linc?"

"Abby, this is your home and I'll not stick my nose into your decisions."

"I can't send a body out in this weather, but then again we can't feed the five of us all winter."

"Then I'll go talk with them." I say, and slowly climb to my feet.

"No, I'll have Jed fetch them in...if you'll retire a ways up the stairs with that rifle of yours."

"I'm to stand guard?" I say, with a half grin.

"You are. You can talk from there if there's anything needs saying." She turns to Jed. "Go invite them in."

In moments both Bama and Twodogs are seated at the table, coffees in hand.

"We have to get some things clear," Abby begins. Neither Bama or Twodogs said a thing, but listened intently. She continued, "I don't want to throw you two out in the weather. When it warms up I suggest you go on over to the Williamson's old place and make yourselves comfortable...it's the only other cabin on this side of the mountain. A little patching and it'll keep the weather off you."

"May I speak, ma'am?" Bama asks.

"Of course," Abby replies.

"I done took a peek in your smokehouse and unless you gots other food, you'll barely make it through an average winter. You keep taking care like you done been and Mister

Twodogs here and me will fill that smokehouse and your wood shed until the weather turns. Where we kilt that cow elk there's another forty or so. Will that suit you, ma'am?"

Abby laughs. "That will, but you have to promise me something."

"Yes'em."

"Should you get a whiff of a posse on the prowl, you'll hightail it out of here and not come back. And while you're in or near my house, you'll stay as innocent as the day your mama first took you to her breast."

Bama smiles, and crosses his heart, then adds, "Ma'am, I didn't do the things they say I done."

"That's between you and the Lord." She turns to Twodogs. "And you, Mister Twodogs. Can you live in peace while here?"

Twodogs nods solemnly.

"Then you gentlemen go about your business and please do your best to stay welcome."

They down their coffee and head for the door. Bama pauses in the doorway. "Ma'am, would you prefer elk, deer, grouse or rabbits. I believe we can fill your smokehouse with what y'all favor."

Abby couldn't help but smile. "Why, Mister Bama, I believe I'll leave that up to you. Possum is about the only critter I can't abide in my kitchen."

"Then possums be off the menu," he closes the door and he and Twodogs go to saddle up.

Chapter Twenty Three

DOB WAS CAREFUL to hire a couple of hooligans who'd give him no trouble, and who'd be more than happy with a few drinks and half what he'd been allowed to pay them. Both had agreed to a dollar a day and food, so he'd keep a buck each.

Torrance O'Toole, a redhead with pork chop sideburns, worked part time as a swamper at the Cattlemen's; and Bernie Switzer, with a full fuzzy black beard, was an unemployed miner—unemployed due to his overfamiliarity with John Barleycorn. 'Tory', as O'Toole was called, had his own nag and when Dob laid eyes on the swayback was glad he really didn't have any intention of going up the mountain into deeper and deeper snow on a real hunt for Dolan and the big black fella, Alabama, or whatever his name was. He hired another fair looking dappled gray from the hostler for Switzer as well as a fine looking black pack mule with gear.

The next morning, still in a heavy drizzle, they rode out of town heading due west just after the mercantile opened so Dob could fill the panniers of the mule, and before Wentworth hit the office so he didn't have to deal with the mean old bastard. He smiled as they cleared the town limits as he'd talked Mayberry, the proprietor, into noting a side of bacon on the list of supplies that would go to the Marshal's office with the invoice rather than the four quarts of hooch he had tucked away.

The two new deputies could barely get the smiles off their faces when given a pair of cheap copper badges proclaiming their new status as lawmen.

They got a mile out of town before Dob swung to the north-west and up the side of the mountain a quarter mile, then due north until he came out on the flat where he reined up and let Tory and Bernie catch up. Tory was leading the pack horse, and immediately started complaining.

"Hell's fire, when is Bernie or you gonna drag this lop-eared nag," he moaned.

"Don't hold yer breath waiting for the boss man to do no nag-draggin'. Bernie can take it for a while." Then he yelled to Bernie, "Come on over here close. I got some instructin' to do."

"I'll bet," Bernie said, with a little sarcasm, and nudged the dappled gray closer.

"Alright, this is the way it is. You two want to slosh through the snow or go onto Juncket Town and that fine establishment they got there."

"Hell's bells," Tory said, with a smile, "Miss Mattie's is fine with me. We gonna get paid for our time there?"

"You'll get your dollar a day, but only if'n you keep your mouth shut." Then he turned to Bernie, "Wentworth is just trying to keep them four city council fellas quiet. You got that clear, no yappin' to nobody, particularly not to the Marshal. We're gonna lay up at Juncket Town, we ain't gonna go up the mountain and get our asses shot off. But only if you two can keep yer lips buttoned tight. I hear one word about it after we get back to Helena and you'll be pushing up daisies. Understand?"

"Suits me," Bernie said. "How stupid do I look to you, Dob? I bet that snow is already four foot deep on top the mountain. Do I look like a guy who'd rather bed down in deep snow or with a fat whore...if you can loan us the price of one against our coming wages?"

"I got a pocket fulla coin. Just remember, buttoned lips."

Both his 'deputies' nodded enthusiastically.

"Then it's Junket Town and Miss Mattie's," Dob said, and reined his steel gray around and gigged him into a quick walk. He glanced over his shoulder at the rising sun, then said to himself as much as the others, "It'll be mid-afternoon a'fore we get there but it ain't hardly no higher than Helena, so we won't have to deal with the damn snow."

Twodogs and Bama, had saddled up and ridden around the mountain in foot deep snow until they came upon fresh tracks of a dozen elk moving down the mountain, then split up and paralleled the track a hundred yards on either side. Only three hundred yards down the mountain, Bama spotted the herd another hundred and fifty yards below bedded down under a nice open copse of fir. He dismounted and tied his animal, pulled the Winchester he'd retrieved from the deputy that Crazy Willy had killed, tested the wind, then moved as carefully and quietly as he could down their way. He was just lining up on a fat cow when a shot rang out and all hell broke loose as the herd was on their feet and stampeding his way. He tried to sight in on a big bull, but he was moving through the trees so he turned his attention to a rag horn, then the crashing behind him made him spin. He fired from the hip at a cow humping up through the snow only twenty feet away. She didn't fall, but continued up the mountain another twenty yards, then spun and started back down. This time he was able to aim and fire and hit her in the vitals. She ran another forty yards before she stacked up against a large fir and lay unmoving.

Only then did Bama glance downhill to see Twodogs slogging through the snow, knife in hand, to a mound of brown fir.

They had two elk down and their work cut out for them for the next three hours or so.

Bama pulled his hunting knife and began gutting the cow, when Twodogs yelled up at him.

"Better work together. Come help."

So, he re-sheathed his knife, shouldered his Winchester and moved down the hill. With two of them working they soon had the small bull Twodogs had dropped gutted, skinned, and were boning the meat with the carcass protected from the snow laying on its own pelt.

With loins and tenderloins removed and rolled up they began each working on a hindquarter, when Twodogs reached over and poked Bama on the shoulder. He looked up with a "What?"

Twodogs pointed back up the mountain to Bama's cow. "Griz not in den yet."

A very large dark grizzly with silver tips on the hair of his hump was rolling the cow over as easily as the men would have rolled a rabbit.

Bama had never seen a griz before, and dropped his knife and grabbed up his Winchester. "Sweet Lord a'mighty," he mumbled, then asked, "what do we do?"

"Hope he run off," Twodogs said, and put a shot near enough to the grizzly that it kicked snow onto his foreleg.

The big bear spun and eyed the two men down the mountain.

"If charge, shoot for shoulder," Twodogs said.

"Shoulder?" Bama asked, not taking his eyes off the huge animal.

"Hard to kill, break shoulders, can't run—"

He barely got it out when the bear took great umbrage at the two paltry looking men, and began an easy lope down the mountain right at them.

Chapter Twenty Four

"SHOULDER," TWODOGS SHOUTED THIS TIME, and fired, followed quickly by Bama's shot. They'd each got two shots off before the bear was on them, knocking two hundred and fifty pound Bama fifteen feet to the side then turning on Twodogs, who got another shot off.

The bear, roaring, whipped his head back and forth, spewing spittle and blood a half dozen feet to each side, rose on his hind legs and with determined but wounded steps, closed the ten feet to where Twodogs stood his ground, who managed to get another shot off—luckily centered in the animal's huge neck.

The bear reached the big Indian and covered him with an embrace that took them both to the ground.

Bama managed to recover his rifle and get another shot off to the bear's vitals, trying his best not to hit Twodogs, now pinned under the bear.

But the shot was unnecessary as the bear was stone cold dead.

Twodogs was trying his best to squirm out from under the weight of the huge animal. Bama moved forward then winced as he saw his fellow hunter almost solid with blood covering his hair, face, and neck.

Bama was finding it difficult to move, realizing he must have one or more broken ribs, and was bleeding from the swipe of the bear's massive paw and three inch claws.

Bama, gasping for air, tried to roll the bear off Twodogs, but couldn't budge him. The animal had to be well over six hundred pounds.

"Get...horse," Twodogs managed.

"You gonna be okay?" Bama asked.

"Blood...mostly...bear," he said, shaking his head back and forth.

"Don't move," Bama said and started up the hill to his animal.

"My horse closer...good rope on saddle," the Indian managed, gasping while talking.

Bama turned and backtracked Twodog's footprints in the snow. He found the paint tied to a fir sapling only seventy-five yards away, and started leading him back. He had to stop and suck wind, wincing with every breath. He thought of mounting the animal, but was afraid he'd pass out with the effort. Gasping with every step, he struggled on.

But he made it, having to calm the horse as the animal wanted nothing to do with the bear. He got him within twenty feet and tied to a sapling, then unstrung the reata, tied it off to the horse's neck, and moved to the bear. He tied it over the bear's back to the far foreleg.

"How you doing?" he asked Twodogs as he worked.

"Har...breath," the Indian managed.

"We'll have him off'n you," Bama said, and moved back to the pinto.

He had no trouble getting the pinto to move away from the smell of the bear. He got a strain on the reata and it stretched tight, then, with Bama slapping the pinto on the rump, the bear rolled.

Bama hurried back as quickly as his screaming ribs would allow, and, finding Twodogs sitting up, helped him to his feet. Then sunk to one knee with the effort.

The Indian eyed the big black. "You hurt bad?"

"Ribs broke. Sliced up a mite."

"I fetch your horse," Twodogs said, and to Bama's surprise moved away up the mountain as if he hadn't just gotten out from beneath a bear that likely weighed half again what he and the Indian would total together.

Bama collapsed, using the bear for a bench, and sat with his face in his hands trying to ease his breathing and smile through the pain.

He was surprised to see Twodogs return without the dun.

"Horse run off. Horse not like bear." He was smiling, and Bama would have too, but all he could think about was his inability to hike up the mountain to the cabin, which had to be more than a mile away, almost all uphill in the snow.

He did manage to smile back at Twodogs. "Smart horse," he said.

"You wait," Twodogs said, then went to work cutting a large swatch of elk hide and rolling the loins and what meat they'd boned from the hindquarters into the hide. Then he cut long thin slices of hide and tied the bundle.

He moved away and collected the pinto and to the horse's nervous objections, led him back to the bear. "Climb up on bear," he instructed Bama, who slowly was able to do so, with one hand on the Indian's shoulder to steady himself. He positioned the pinto so Bama could get a foot in the stirrup then shoved him up in the saddle.

Then he hoisted the fat bundle of meat up in front of him.

"I lead," Twodogs said. "You hang on. No drop meat."

"Right," Bama mumbled, then bit a lip as Twodogs set off up the mountain. "Gonna be a long trip."

Dob, Tory, and Bernie rode into Junket City mid-afternoon. Dob, riding in the front and letting the other two ride drag, was not aware that Bernie, on the trail, had been regularly hoisting a pint of Last Chance Panther Piss, distilled in Helena in a small room behind Paddy's Saloon by Rosco, a bartender and distiller who prided himself on the highest proof whiskey west of the Mississippi...or so he claimed.

Junket City was a failed Silver Strike, so only a third of the two dozen clapboard and log structures were occupied. But Mattie's, known far and wide in the territory as Miss Mattie's Parlor and Pleasure House, was a destination for the miners in the nearby mountains, a few river men who operated above the Great Falls, and every drover who had a dollar in his pocket for a poke and the free pint of whiskey Mattie threw in should you invest in a second token when you recovered from the first.

As they neared the scruffy little town, Dob looked back over his shoulder when he heard the tinkle of breaking glass, and realized that Bernie had finished a pint bottle and thrown it into the rocks beside the trail.

"Damn fool," Dob muttered under his breath.

Only two businesses thrived in Junket City. Mattie's, the only two story structure in town, and Ogglebee's, a small but well stocked mercantile.

There were more than a dozen horses tied up at the rail in front of Mattie's two story saloon and bawdy house. The lower half was logs and sturdy, and as her business grew she'd removed the roof and built a clapboard second story, then reused the roof material from the former one story business...Mattie believed in waste-not, want-not. And it served her well.

They dismounted, loosened the cinches on the horses and pack mule, dropped the panniers under the hitching rail, and headed for the batwing doors. Dob stopped them before they pushed through.

"You two take them copper badges off and we're gonna tell these folks we're from way down Bozeman way, understand?"

"Let's get in there, I'm dry as a desert road apple and so hungry my stomach is flapping against my backbone," said Tory,

"Bullshit, you listen."

"We can palaver over a shot of hooch."

"I said listen. I don't want no trouble so you two hang your gun belts on your saddle horns or stuff them in the panniers."

"How about you?" Tory asked.

"I'm the actual law here, but I'm gonna pocket my badge and we're not gonna let anyone know we're from just over the hill at Helena, understand.

Both the boys nodded, bent down and quickly stuffed their gun belts in the panniers, then headed for the batwings.

"Hold up," Dob said, stopping them again, "there's more."

Chapter Twenty Five

"WE'RE GONNA BE HERE AT least three days. You boys will have four dollars each a'comin' to you. And your old buddy, Dob, here, will advance you them dollars and 'cause I'm such a good sort I'll only charge you four bits for the loan...so you'll get three fifty and owe me four days work...including today a'course as I'm a fair sort."

"Four bits...," Bernie said, scratching his head. "That don't...don't hardly...seem fair, Dob." As he was a half head shorter than Dob, he glared up at the man.

Dob could see Bernie was in his cups as he was slurring his words. "Okay, then at the end of each day I'll pay you the dollar you got coming."

"Can I have today's dollar now?" Bernie said, a little whine in his voice.

"Hell no, come bedtime I'll pay you the dollar."

"But all I got is two bits."

Tory stepped forward, "I'll take my three fifty now."

Bernie was fuming. "Damn you, Dob. You ain't emperor Napoleon, you're a low life som'bitch. You're a'trying to cheat us."

"Bernard, I don't want to see your ugly mug until it's time for me to pony up a dollar—"

"No, sir," Bernie said, calming a bit. "I believe I'll take my three dollars and fifty cents now. I heard tell there's a cocoa brown pleasure lady here, and I sure as hell don't wanna take seconds to the likes of you two."

Arguing with Bernie was not nearly as profitable as only paying him three dollars and fifty cents for four days work, so Dob bit his tongue and coughed up the money, with the admonition, "Don't y'all come back beggin' me for more. I don't give a damn if you poked or drunk away all your money and are starving. You understand?"

Bernie and Tory both nodded, then spun on their booted heels and headed for the Brunswick carved walnut bar that was long enough to accommodate a dozen customers. Goober peanut shells covered the floor and a hogshead barrel rested in the middle of the room, heaped full of whole nuts. Half the occupants puffed on pipes or cigars and smoke lingered down from the ceiling to head height.

There were a good dozen men on stools and two standing at each end of the bar, as well as two round tables with four at one at six at the other. Drovers, miners and a couple who looked to be drummers were laughing and yucking it up, each trying to better the story of the other while entertaining three soiled doves. Two of them were ladies of generous girth, one with breasts the size of melons and the other, an older lady, of equal size but deflated. An upright piano rose against one wall but its bench sat empty.

The third dove, half the size of the other two, sat on a table with four men gathered around her. Two of the men had plates full of beans and beef.

Bernie elbowed between a couple of fellas in canvas trousers and striped shirts with neckerchiefs and wide-brimmed hats. Both were heeled, one with a Bowie knife in addition to a heavy revolver. The other wore a six shooter on his left side, butt forward for a right hand cross draw. They eyed Bernie up and down, which didn't take long as he was a head shorter than one and a half-head than the other. Seeming to take some offense, one of them rested a hand on his revolver, but as Bernie paid them no attention, they went back to their conversation, talking over his head.

The bartender was a barrel-chested fellow with one pearl eye and a scar across it from forehead to chin, making half that eyebrow offset a half-a-brow from the other half. The scar would have originated from his hair line had he any hair, but he only had greasy tufts over his ears. He wiped the bar down as he spotted Bernie and came his way.

"What's yer pleasure?" he asked, his voice a low growl and deep as a well.

"The cost of a bottle of whiskey?"

"Five dollars for the good stuff down to a dollar for the stuff with no label."

"And a beer?"

"A thin dime."

"You take dust?" Tory asked, not that he had any.

The bartender glanced over his shoulder to the small scale with its tiny weights on the back bar. "What's that look like to you, stranger? It ain't for measuring the weight of your manhood. We charge a dollar for a token, no matter how little a two gram dick you got. Now, what the hell ya drinking. Winter's coming on."

"You're a funny som'bitch for being so damned ugly. What's yer name so I know who I'm insultin'?" Bernie said, curling a lip at the big man. Bernie was wearing a fur-out coat that made him look bigger than his diminutive frame, and puffed his chest and tried to look more than pint size.

The bartender wasn't impressed. "The last little sawed off fart that insulted me is feedin' the worms. Are you trying to join him?"

Bernie was uncharacteristically quiet for a moment, then asked, "How 'bout one of them dime beers?"

"Make it two," Tory said, who'd elbowed up behind him.

"And a whiskey," Dob said from over his shoulder. He, too, had elbowed between the two cowhands.

"By God you fellas are pushy," the larger of the two cowhands said in a low growl.

Revenge of the Damned

Dob, equally tall if not as thick, turned and eyeballed the man, "You two were blockin' the bar. Unless'n you own this place, you need to make way."

The man ignored him and spoke over Tory's shoulder to his pard, "Rafe, let's move over and take us a chair. It's gettin' a little whiffy hereabouts."

The two of them moved away from the bar and across the room to where two ladder back chairs backed up to a stairway to the upper story.

Dob worked up his most fearsome glare, which wasn't much from a tall skinny fella with an Adam's apple the size of an apricot. But he stared at them all the way as they crossed the room, then glanced up as he and every man in the place quieted. The woman descending the stairs was as beautiful as Jenny Lind if a lot darker. In fact, cocoa colored, yet she had wine red hair that hung to the center of her back, and her back was half bare but not attracting nearly so many stares as the flawless brown breasts that pushed up out of a regal purple-colored lace-trimmed gown. And, to Dob's surprise, as he watched her step from the last riser to the saloon floor, she had emerald eyes, not the ebony ones one would expect from a dark-skinned woman.

"By all that's holy," Dob said, under his breath, "that's the most woman of all the women my eyes have enjoyed lookin' on in all my thirty-three years."

"Damn if she ain't," Bernie managed, backhanding the foam from his mustache and beard. "Even if'n her daddy bedded a nigra."

"May be the only time ever I agree with you two, but I agree," Tory said.

"Gentlemen," she said, with a voice that carried over the room, "what would you like to hear?" And she floated over to the piano where two miners about came to blows trying to pull the bench out for her.

"Settle down, if you want a song," she said, batting her eyes at the two, who both smiled wide enough that they each showed missing teeth.

"Now, requests?" she asked, looking back over her shoulders as long fingers, with colored fingernails, covered the keys.

A half dozen requests rang out from the crowd, and she began to play *Greensleeves*, and a few of the men went back to playing cards or talking, then she broke into song and the place quieted again, only coming to life after she was well into the old English ballad.

Dob moved up against the bar and waved the bartender over. "That a pleasure lady?" he asked the big man with one eye.

"That's Belle, Miss Marie Bellerose, and yes, if you pass her muster and have the pair of tokens—"

"Pair?"

"Two dollars worth. She might indulge you for twenty minutes or so."

"Twenty minutes. You think I'm a rabbit?"

"Most fellas don't get past just watchin' her disrobe, which is one of the great pleasures in a fella's life. In fact just seeing that big bed of hers is worth a token. She has a room half the size of this, up front, and she's got a porch with some fine chairs and table to take her breakfast on when weather's agreeable, with a view of the big mountain."

As he eyed her, another woman, older, but easy on the eyes, came down the stairs, with a cowhand close behind.

"Who's that whore?" Dob asked the bartender.

The big man glared at him. "That's my wife, Miss Mattie to you. And if you want to swallow them ugly teeth, you keep rattling them talking ugly."

"Why, she just come down the stairs with a cowhand."

"She's a working woman too, a pleasure lady, but you mind your mouth, or I won't allow any of them to bed the likes of you."

Dob shrugged and watched the woman who gave the big bartender a wink, then disappeared into a back room.

Dob just shook his head and wondered if any woman could be worth a full day's pay, no matter how perfect brown she was and how big a room she had.

But he meant to find out.

Chapter Twenty Six

BAMA SELDOM COMPLAINED about pain or discomfort.

He'd escaped a plantation in Alabama and made his way north at the beginning of what the southerners call 'the unpleasantries' until he joined up with the Southard's Company in Pennsylvania. He fought across the south, and twice wounded, finally healed, mustered out, and made his way to the Tennessee River and a job on a sidewheeler down the Tennessee to the Ohio, the Ohio to the Mississippi, then up to the Missouri and another long trip up it to Fort Benton. Then a job with a mule train freighting outfit as he had it in his mind to see the Pacific Ocean. He'd seen more that his fair share of pain and gore, but he was moaning loud enough to rattle the small panes of glass in Abby Quinn's cabin by the time Twodogs led his paint up to the door, and rapped.

Abby peeked out of one of those panes then yelled at Jed, who was up in the loft studying. "Jed, come running. Mister Bama appears to be hurt...bad."

I was shaken awake, while resting on my pallet. As she threw the door open, I carefully rose to a sitting position, then using my Golden Boy for a crutch stood as Jed arrived at her side.

"Take meat," I hear Twodogs say, and Abby steps outside and takes the large furry bundle of meat from in front of Bama.

"Need help," Twodogs says, and Jed steps around to the left side of the paint to help catch Bama who is trying to swing a leg over the paint's rump.

Revenge of the Damned

"What happened," Abby asks, after setting the meat inside the cabin.

"Bear want elk. Need boy go back with me."

"Where's Mister Bama's horse?" Abby asks.

Twodogs points to where the Dun stands on the far side of the corral, his head over the rail, nuzzling her palomino mare. "Come home," Twodogs says.

"Let's get Mr. Bama into the barn so I can take a look at him."

"Cut bad on side. Need sewing up."

"I can do that," she says, and joins Twodogs and Jed in helping to guide the big man's horse toward the barn. When they get to the door she goes inside where she hurriedly makes a bed by rearranging some saddle blankets over a hastily thrown layer of meadow hay. As she works she calls instructions out the open door, "Jed, build the fire up, then fetch my sewing basket from the cabin. And a couple of my clean kitchen towels. And the jug, so we can douse his wounds."

"Yes, 'em," the boy says, entering the barn, and hurriedly feeds some small firewood into the mouth of the pot belly stove, then runs for the cabin.

"Then saddle horses," Twodogs yelled after him. "All horses, two pack, two ride. We need fetch meat. Two elk and bear wait."

"Dead bear I hope," Abby says, worriedly.

"Bear dead, two elk dead." Twodogs says, with as close to a grin as he ever gets.

Twodogs and Abby slowly help Bama out of the saddle then quickly into the barn as he moans in pain. "Not cuts hurtin' so bad," he said, "broke ribs,"

"Well," Abby responds, "I can't do much about your ribs, but we can work on the cuts." She pulls his shirt up and gasps a little, then says, turning to Twodogs. "I hope this meat didn't come too dear."

"He tough. He heal. Meat good, but hurry before more bear or wolves."

"Hurry, Jed," she says, under her breath, reinforcing Twodogs request, then turns to the big Indian. "You take good care with my boy, Mister Twodogs. You don't want this Irish mother coming to get even with you. If anything bad happens to Jed I promise you'd rather fight a bear than me."

Twodogs merely shrugs. He wasn't used to a woman confronting him in any way, but he'd long ago decided he would never understand the way the white eyes lived.

Jed returns with Abby's sewing basket, with me limping along behind. As she readies a needle and thread, I kneel down beside Bama with a towel in hand. I sop the blood away from four deep cuts raking the big man's side as she works.

"Only use one towel," Abby instructs. "We'll need the second for a clean dressing."

"Yes, ma'am," I say with a slight smile. I like the way she takes over when it comes to nursing.

I reach over and pick up the whiskey. "We'll save some for dousing," I say, then add, "but he'll need some for courage."

"Save me a couple of inches," she says, as I lift Bama up high enough that he can drink. After giving him four big mouthfuls, I lay him back down and pick up an inch-thick branch from the wood pile and shove it between Bama's teeth. "Gnaw on this. It'll at least keep you from cussin' us."

Bama nods, eyes wide, not seeing much humor in the situation and he clamps down hard as Abby grabs the jug and douses and cleans his wounds with the whiskey.

Then she begins stitching him up.

He doesn't flinch, or whimper as she works, but his jaw is clamped and jaw muscles bulge. She dresses the wounds with the clean towel then uses his shirt to tie the towel tight to his flesh. He moans when she pulls it tight, but from the ribs screaming at him, not the cuts.

"Thank you, ma'am," he manages. "Fine job, I be bettin'."

"If the bleeding stops and it doesn't go green it's a fine job," she says, then rises and turns to me. "You stay with him and make sure he doesn't bleed more. And keep the fire going strong. I'm going to fetch some food for Jed and Mister Twodogs. Sounds like they've got their work cut out."

When she walks out of the barn into the foot of snow, she sees that Jed and the Indian are mounting up, each with an animal in tow. I hear her yell at them through the door, "Hold up, I'll fetch you some supper to take along."

I shake my head as I lean back against the barn wall and watch Bama try to sleep.

Damn if that ain't one hell of a woman, and what a fine man that Jed will grow to be. In moments, Bama is snoring quietly. Occasionally moaning low, but sleeping.

It looks as if me and the Quinns will have plenty of company all winter, and plenty of meat for the smokehouse should Jed and Twodogs get back with all they'd gone to recover. It'll take at least three trips, I guess, and grouse that I'm not fit to go with them. Another week, I figure, and I'll be moving and ready to sit a saddle. God willin' and the posse don't come.

I'll have plenty of company for the winter, but also lots more prey hanging around to attract the law—wanted men all—and, even in a week, I won't be ready to light out in front of a posse.

Chapter Twenty Seven

IT TOOK DOB ANOTHER FIVE beers and five shots of cheap whiskey to get the courage to elbow his way through the miners, cowhands and drummers to sidle up to Miss Belle.

He didn't bother to remove his hat, after all he was talking with a whore, no matter how beautiful she might be.

"Bartender...tolt me," he was slurring his words, "it was two...two tokens to give y'all a poke. That right?"

Belle turned slowly on the bench to face Dob, and flashed a smile at him that lit up the room. "Why, kind sir, thank you for the offer, but I do believe I'll keep on entertaining all my friends."

She gave him her back.

"I'll give y'all one token." He mumbled.

Without turning, she politely refused again. "That's a fine offer, sir. But I believe not."

"All right, damn you...two tokens. But that's for...for an hour."

Again, she didn't bother to turn around, and merely began a lively tune, still giving him her back, totally ignoring him. Insulting him like he wasn't her better.

Dob reached out, grabbing her by the shoulder and spinning her around. "Get yer black ass...upstairs. I'm gonna...gonna see if you're worth a damn dollar."

Before she could answer, a miner stepped out of the crowd and put a hard right across the side of Dob's jaw, spinning him into the crowd, where another hit him equally hard, and then another, and another, until he went down. Then a cowhand kicked him hard in the ribs, then another from the other side. Then a pair of miners on one side and a pair of cowhands on the other, picked him up by the arms and legs and ran him head first through the batwing doors, smashing through them, and heaving him out into the dirt street.

They turned and headed back into the saloon, laughing and brushing their hands together as if they'd been handling a sack of cow manure.

As they returned, Belle gave them a special smile and asked, "Any special requests, fellas?"

Bernie and Tory had not made a move to help their drunken employer, as they were equally drunk, and had never been inclined to get their heads busted, particularly for someone they figured had cheated them on every turn.

"What'cha think, Bernie?" Tory asked, as soon as things had settled down in the saloon.

"'Bout what?" Tory mumbled.

"'Bout Dob. You think they done kilt him?"

"Na, he's way to hardheaded for a couple of hard knocks to even dent his noggin...but maybe you should go check."

"Me? How about you checkin'."

"I ain't finished my beer."

"Me neither. Let's go together when we're finished up," Bernie said, then had another thought. "He's likely got a pocket fulla coin...least ways he done said he did."

Tory slugged down the rest of his beer. "Best we check on ol' Dob."

"Best we do," Bernie said, and upended his, then they headed for the batwings.

"Damn," Tory said as they pushed their way through.

Dob was sitting up in the street holding his sides, bleeding from his nose, a cut over his eye, and from both ears.

The two walked out into the dirt road and both placed hands on knees, bending close to Dob.

"You okay," Bernie asked.

"Wa happen...what happened," Dob asked.

"You musta said sumpin' to that fine-looking woman what made them fellas inside a little angry at you."

"That black whore...she...she put 'em on me. Must have been two...two damn dozen," he managed, rubbing his jaw as he did.

"Nope," Tory said, "only four. But they was big ones."

Then Dob suddenly came to the realization that his two deputies had been no help. "And what the hell was you two imbeciles a'doin' while they was beating me in the head with clubs."

"No clubs," Bernie said. "We charged in and they grabbed us up and said they wasn't gonna kill you, but said they'd kill us if'n we interfered, also we was unarmed and they was all heeled."

Dob glanced from one to the other. "If'n I hadn't done paid you fools in advance I'd fire you. Help me up."

They each grabbed him under an arm, and pulled him up to his feet. He wavered a moment, then stumbled over to his horse, stopped, and turned back. "You two worthless turds tighten up my cinch and let's go out and find a place to camp."

"There's an old barn at the edge of town," Tory said. "Ain't nobody around there and it'll keep the rain off'n us. It looks like it's gonna get ugly, maybe even sleet or snow."

"Wait," Dob said, as they were about to help him up into the saddle. He reached in a pocket and handed Bernie a silver dollar. "Go back in there and buy me a bottle of whiskey. I need me some pain killer."

"You gonna share?" Bernie asked.

"I'm not gonna share an ounce of lead with your dumb ass. You get in there and get me a bottle."

Bernie shrugged and stumbled back into the bar.

***

Twodogs and Jed had made two trips with packsaddles and elk-hide bags hung from their saddles, and on the third they were loaded with the prime cuts from the bear. More than half the bear meat was still on the bone, but the hide they'd hoisted up into a tree so some critter didn't drag it off. It would make a fine rug or winter coat after a couple of months scraping and curing with a mixture of ash and the animal's own brains made into a tanning mash.

Abby was at the door staring out worriedly when they rode slowly into the meadow and crossed the creek. Bama was sleeping, best he could in the barn. It had warmed some in the afternoon, enough to cause a bit of a thaw, and the trickle of a creek was now knee high on the horses.

They crossed without incident and rode straight to the smokehouse, where Abby, with some help from me, had been hanging meat to smoke and slicing the worst cuts to dry for jerky.

"Thank God," she says, looking over her shoulder to where I'm back on the pallet.

"All good?" I ask, peering up.

"All good," she replies. "How about elk liver and onions."

"That should get us all in fine fettle," I say, giving her a wide smile. Then I realize, I've smiled more in the last few days than I have since I joined the Union to do my part in preserving her.

And it wasn't just because of Abby's great cooking, but it sure didn't hurt.

Chapter Twenty Eight

DOB'S HEAD THROBBED and he ached all over, and he was growing more angry with every swig from the bottle. His bedroll was nestled in a pile of hay and inviting, but he couldn't sleep, thinking of the black bitch who'd shamed him. If he was back on his daddy's farm in Louisiana, he'd have had her hung from the nearest oak. After, of course, he'd had his way with her.

What, he wondered, would hurt her more than hanging her from an oak, which would only end her misery? Her looks, that was what all vain women valued more than money or fame or their man or family. Her looks, that's what he'd take. Maybe he'd cut off her teats and make himself a tobacco pouch from one.

He'd been drinking in the barn more than two hours, and the bottle was half gone. Both Tory and Bernie were snoring loud enough to wake the dead, not that he needed their help.

He dug his small four-inch folding knife out of his pocket and tested the edge, then pulled his boots back on, ran an arm into each sleeve of Tory's coat as it was big enough to fit him. It was old and tattered but was made of coyote hides flanking a wolverine hide with a pair of white stripes down the back. It had been a beautiful coat at some long past time. Very distinctive, and if he was seen by anyone, they'd think Tory was to blame.

He slipped out the backdoor of the barn into a heavy rain, then kept behind a row of empty buildings until he was nearing

Revenge of the Damned

Mattie's. The place was silent. He made his way down between the saloon-bordello and the building next door and peeked at the street. Not a horse left at the hitching rail, not a lantern or candle showing lit inside. He stepped up on the boardwalk and crossed to the bat wings, and found two heavy doors closed and locked inside them.

He scratched his head. Then realized the building to the side was built right up against Mattie's, and its windows were broken out and its door was hanging on one hinge and standing open. He moved quietly to it and slipped inside. It was a false-front building, as many were in these hit-and-miss come-and-go mining towns, and had sturdy log rafters with a tattered canvas roof. It had been not much more than a hard-walled tent, when it harbored a saloon that hadn't been one forth the size of Mattie's.

But the plank bar still stood.

Dob moved to it and climbed up atop it, giving him only five more feet to the top of the wall connecting the building to Mattie's. He slipped the folding knife out and cut a flap in the canvas roof, then hoisted himself up. There were no windows on his side of Mattie's, but he easily made his way forward to the slightly sloped deck that served as Mattie's roof over the boardwalk and doubled as Belle's porch in the front of the two-story place. He waited at the rail of the deck and listened for a long while. No lights came from what he presumed was the Belle woman's big room, nor was there any sound.

He hoisted a leg over the rail and slipped past a window to a door centered in the wide wall near a round table with four chairs. The bartender had mentioned that Belle had a table on her porch. Another window to match the first was on the far side.

Wondering if he could be so lucky, he tried the door. No reason to lock a door out to a porch that had no stairway...and he'd guessed right, as the knob turned, and the door swung in as he pushed ever so slowly.

There was enough moonlight that he could make out a bed, a four poster, with cloth enclosures pulled back. There was a hump under the covers, and he smiled to himself and moved forward until he could see that wine-colored hair spread over a pillow and hear her breathing.

He took a deep calming breath, then threw the covers back. He leapt up and threw a leg over the woman—damn if she didn't sleep in the raw—and straddled her, pinning one of her arms. He slammed his other hand over her mouth as she gasped and before she could scream.

She wiggled and fought him with her one free hand but had little effect as she was beneath him and his long arm kept her nails away from his face.

He had to shift his weight and let loose her captured hand so he could reach in his pocket to retrieve the folding knife, and when he did she began hitting and scratching him with both her hands. He got it unfolded and smacked her hard across the side of the head with the blunt end of the knife.

She sunk her teeth into the hand covering her mouth and he jerked it back, allowing her to scream. His hand was bleeding badly and anger coursed his backbone and flushed his cheeks. He cocked his arm back making a fist, and smashed his wounded hand into her face.

"Bastard," she managed, and he sliced at her with the knife, opening her face from in front of an ear to her chin.

He was rearing back to slice her again, when the flash of gunfire and sound of a shot shocked him, then pain shot through him and he threw himself off her.

Standing in shock for a moment he realized she had a double-barrel belly gun in hand, and his shirt was holed and smoking from a contact shot. The bitch had a pistol under her pillow. And someone was pounding on the door, yelling her name.

Holding his bleeding side he spun and ran for the door to the porch, was going through it, as the top of the frame splintered just above his head from her second barrel, and outside and over the rail as the door between room and hall smashed open.

Dob vaulted the rail, dropped to the street, and ran, ignoring the pain in his side, then ran even faster as another shot rang out and mud splattered beside him. He cut to the side and between two buildings and was out of sight of the saloon.

Barney, the big one-eyed bartender hurried back into the room where Mattie was applying a towel as a compress to the slice on Belle's face. Belle was sobbing, and the room filled with the other three soiled doves who shared rooms on the second floor.

"Who did this," Barney snapped as soon as they got the bleeding quelled with the compress.

"Fur out coat," Belle managed.

"He have a full black beard?" Barney asked.

"Too dark, couldn't tell," Belle managed.

"I saw him running away. I'm heading over to the boarding house and gettin' some help, then I'm going after that prick. I remember that coat. And that face. We'll get him."

Belle walked out with him. "I'm going to get some more clean dressings. Barney, you get that son of a bitch and hang him from a high limb. He's ruined a beautiful girl...and cost us a hell of a lot of money. We were averaging four dollars a day off Belle. But that likely won't happen again. Hang that bastard, for you and me...and Belle."

"It'll be my pleasure," Barney growled and strode away with determination.

Chapter Twenty Nine

DOB WENT STRAIGHT BACK to the barn, draped the fur coat over Bernie's feet, then to the attached corral where his animal was harbored. He saddled up and rode out of town back towards Helena, keeping a neckerchief pressed tightly to the flesh wound on his bleeding side. Bernie and Tory snored away in their bedrolls, peacefully sleeping off the beers they'd swilled at Mattie's.

Barney, the one-eyed bartender, went to the only boarding house in town and strode in and began banging on doors. He soon had a half dozen men following, and all saddled up and following him as he moved out of town to the south...but he reined up when he passed the old abandoned barn and saw two horses in the normally empty corral.

He and two of the rapidly formed posse dismounted, tied their animals to the fence rail and headed inside, guns drawn. Barney carried a Winchester.

They moved to the remnants of a haystack and saw two men curled up on their bedrolls.

And draped over the feet one of them, was the unique fur coat.

"By all that's holy," Barney said, "the damn fool done curled up and went to sleep."

They gathered the two men's firearms and only then did Barney give the sleeping man with the full black beard a kick, a hard kick to the ribs."

"What...what the hell," Bernie managed as Tory too, sat up, trying to clear his eyes.

"Roll over on your bellies," Barney commanded.

"What the hell," Tory said, trying to get to his feet.

Barney smashed the butt of his Winchester up against a red pork chop sideburn and Tory went down on his face, unmoving.

"Hey," Bernie yelled, and Barney sliced the stock of the Winchester across his face and he went to his side on the ground, holding a bleeding cut on the cheekbone. "You som'bitch," he managed, but the big bartender stepped into him and drove a boot into his chest with a kick that almost lifted him off the ground. One of the cowhands who'd accompanied him fell on Bernie with a pigging string and tied his wrists behind him, then jerked the belt off the unconscious Tory and circled his elbows and bound them together behind him. Then they yelled for help and others hurried in and they jerked the two men to their feet.

You could hear the anger in Barney's voice as he commanded, "Get bridles on their horses. Don't worry about saddles...they won't need them."

They got the two prisoners up on the barebacks of their horses and two of the posse members led them back to Mattie's.

Barney hurried in and up the stairs to Belle's room, and shouted to the women inside, "Get Belle out to the rail. I want her to see this." Then he spun on his heel and back down the stairs and outside.

Across the road from Mattie's were the remnants of the Baptist Church, long shuttered, long vacant. But the Fir that had been there for far longer than the town still thrived in its small front yard.

"Thirteen turns," Barney yelled at the man who was knotting the end of a pair of reatas.

When Bernie and Tory came to enough to realize what was happening, they began to scream and beg. Ropes were flung over the lowest of the major limbs of the fir, only ten feet off the ground as Barney kicked what was left of a two foot high picket fence away. They led the horses into the small churchyard under the tree as Tory prayed at the top of his lungs.

"Our father, who art in heaven..."

Bernie managed to fling himself off the horse but was quickly subdued by blows, and hoisted back on, with a rope around his neck. Now if he flung himself off, he'd hang.

With both the men mounted and ropes with hangman's knots looped around their throats, Barney looked over his shoulder to see Mattie on one side of Belle and one of the younger pleasure ladies on the other, and he yelled. "You watching this, Belle?"

But Belle was still in shock, and diverted her eyes. She mumbled to Mattie, "Shouldn't we have a trial?"

Mattie snapped at her, "I heard the judge was murdered over in Helena and it'll be a month or more before we get another. These no-accounts will be cold in their grave long before he could get here."

"But I'm not sure—" Belle complained, but it was too late, as the horses were whipped and they bolted out from under Bernie and Tory. They were two low for the fall to break their necks, so they swung and kicked, which only accentuated their swinging...until the kicking slowed as they choked to death. Finally, as all watched the macabre scene, the arch of their swing slowed until they hung, unmoving.

Everyone in the yard or on the porch at Mattie's stood in dead silence, until Belle began sobbing and spun and ran back to her bloodied bed. The women stopped her and one embraced her as others stripped the bedding away.

The men in the yard started to lower Bernie and Tory, but Barney snapped at them, "Let the pricks hang. I want to watch 'em rot for a while."

But the next morning, Mattie insisted they be cut down and hauled to the small cemetery where only a dozen or so had been buried during the town's short four-year life as a boom town.

She told Barney it was bad for business to have a couple of rotting bodies just across the road and particularly in the front yard of a church. No one bothered to build them a pine box. They merely chucked them in shallow graves and threw dirt in their faces.

Dob spent the night sleeping under a low hanging fir only a few miles from Helena. He awoke and checked his backtrail, wondering if there was a posse dogging him.

He was in the office by the time Wentworth arrived at nearly ten AM, with a clean shirt covering his aching wound. And he ached all over from the beating.

"You got them murderers in my cell?" he asked as he walked in and saw Dob sipping coffee.

"No sir," Dob said, spitting out a story he'd been working on during the ride into town. "Damn no-accounts I hired bolted, whilst I was in the bushes taking care of my morning's necessaries, and ran for the hills. They was spooked soon as they realized the snow was getting deep. Tried to get me to quit, but you know me boss...ain't no quit nor back up in me."

"What the hell happened to your face?" Wentworth asked, studying him closely.

"Damn horse bolted and tangled we up with a tree."

Wentworth eyed him carefully, then snapped, "You damn fool, you shoulda hired some decent fellas. I heard you hired a couple of no-accounts. You got what you deserved. You got any of their money left over?"

"I got four dollars."

"Give it up and get your dumb ass to making rounds. Half the city council and the mayor is off to Fort Benton to meet the riverboat. We got a new judge coming this way."

"That was quick," Dob said, looking a little surprised.

"Seems he was already on his way to take Stanley's place. Stop by the Independent and pick up some flyers I had printed."

"Flyers?"

"Yep, reward posters. Five hundred reward for that nigra, Alabama, and five hundred for that knot headed murdering Irishman, Dolan. And a twenty-five dollar one for information on the whereabouts of that Crow, Twodogs."

"I thought he was dog meat."

"I got reason to believe he kilt our barber and I want to catch him and twist his tail until he fesses up. Turns out his pony went missing from the livery the same night as the barber was kilt."

"Hell, I'll take that twenty five right now. That Crow is headed back to Big Horn country to tie up with his tribe. I bet he's had enough of white folks."

"Just get the posters."

Dob shrugged and waved over his shoulder as he headed out, his other hand pressed to the burning wound in his side.

He sucked in a deep breath upon his return, as Wentworth was deep in a conversation with one of the drummers Dob had seen in Mattie's. He almost turned and ran, but thought better of it when Wentworth glanced over. "You got my posters?"

"Yes, sir."

"Ride five miles out of town toward Great Falls on the Mullan's and post one in plain sight of the road, then tomorrow head west and do the same. Put one outside on the bulletin board and one in every saloon in town. Drop a half dozen of each at the express company and tell them they got four dollars coming from the city, a dollar for delivering one of each to the Marshal in Great Falls, Bozeman, Benton City and Deer Lodge. You got that?"

As he was being lectured Dob couldn't help but glance at the Drover, who was giving him a curious look.

He overheard the drover ask the Marshal as he headed for the door, "That fella wasn't up to Junket, was he?"

Marshal Oscar Wentworth shook his head in answer to the drover's question. "Dob's been up the mountain. Now, tell me about these two fellas got strung up and this whore got herself sliced?"

Dob shut the door quietly behind himself. He glanced down at his hands and almost passed out as he realized he had blood under his fingernails.

He went straight to a horse trough, and even as cold as it was with two inches of snow on the ground, he scrubbed until all signs of blood were gone.

Chapter Thirty

I CLIMB OUT OF THE PILE of skins and gimp over and add a couple of logs to the fire.

Abby glances up from her seat at the table, where she is writing a letter to a sister in Illinois. Her look turns to worry. "Lincoln Dolan, I'm not sure you won't pop one of those wounds open. Be careful."

"Yes, ma'am, but I'm getting house bound and I got to move around."

"Around where?"

"Out to the barn, to putter about. I'm not good at this doing nothing."

She smiles at me. "Would you be good at dying right here in my cabin, or out in the barn?"

I smile back at her. "I wouldn't do that to y'all. You'd have to dig in that damn ol' frozen ground."

"Your language, sir," she says, but I know she's teasing me.

"Darn ol' frozen ground."

"That would be a chore."

We are both silent for a moment as she watches me pull my trousers off a hook near my pallet, and take a seat and pull them on over my long Johns.

"Mister Dolan, you off to chop wood, or what?" she asks.

I laugh. "Don't think I'm ready for the woodpile quite yet. But I can putter around in the barn."

"Wait until I get back," she says, and moves around the table and into her room. She returns with a knit sweater and a heavy wool coat, and hands them to me.

"Your husband's?" I ask.

"Going to waste in my cedar chest. Yours now."

"You sure?" I ask.

"Sure as the sun rising in the east."

"And you don't think Jed will get his hackles up...me wearing his pa's things."

She's quiet for a moment, then glances shyly at me. "Linc, if you're going to be here for the winter, and I hope longer, and if you're feeling up to it, I..." She's silent for another moment, and I don't move a muscle.

So she continues. "I've taken a shine to you. Quite a shine."

"And I to you, Abby."

"I want you to consider staying on...after you're well, long after the snow's gone."

It's my turn to be silent for a moment. "You can't afford a hired hand."

"You're teasing me, Mister Dolan."

"Abby, you're a beautiful woman with a fine son. You can do better than this shot-up worn-out wanted man. You go into Helena and they'll be lined up around the block to court you."

"We could leave here, as soon as you're well enough. Maybe go on west, all the way to Washington. I'd like to see the ocean."

Again, silence. Then, determined, I suggest, "If I can clear this mess up in town, and that will be difficult as it's not over by a long shot, I still have a long row to hoe in Helena."

"You have to have revenge...for the death of your fiancé?"

"Abby, she and I hardly knew each other after so long a time apart. And she'd married another. But she didn't deserve to die...to be murdered. And murdered by a man with a badge, a man of the law who no one will fault for what he did. I'm going to kill him, or be killed trying, so I'm no catch for you and Jed."

"You said you were...were with her in a room at the Cattlemen's. That didn't rekindle...."

"That was spite on her part and mostly curiosity on mine...and maybe, admittedly, some pure old lust. But it got her murdered and I can't abide that."

"You killed in the war."

I smiled sadly. "Many times, some close enough I could smell the sweat on them. But I didn't like it and it was war. In fact, I hated it."

"Then hate this revenge you're seeking."

"That's different, Abby. I'm the only one who'll right that wrong. And a good woman died...because of me."

"You didn't lure her up those stairs?"

"No, I did not, but she came because of me."

"You sure you should pay for her spiteful actions."

"It still was me, and I can't set that aside."

She stands and moves to the Buck Stove and returns with a kettle and two cups. "A cup of coffee will warm you up if you're dead set about going out to the barn. You can take Bama a cup of hot coffee." She pours, then eyes me carefully. "If you're going to die come the thaw, or be sent away to prison for the rest of your life, then I want what time we have. I want you to move into my room."

I have to chew on that for a moment, then ask, "And Jed?"

"Jed is upstairs with his studies. I'll have a talk—"

Jed's voice rings out from up in the loft. "It's fine by me. And take pa's clothes. They ain't doing no one no good in ma's chest and it'll be a coon's age a'fore they'll fit me...if ever."

"They're not," Abby scolded, "not they ain't, and it's any good, not no good. And you stop listening in on other's conversations, young man."

"Yes, ma'am, but it did involve me."

"That it did," I say with a wide smile.

Revenge of the Damned

"So," Abby says, her pretty eyebrows raised, "can I clean up this mess of skins off my living room floor."

"I'll fold them up—" I offer.

"You wander out to the barn, and you be careful in the doing of it."

"Yes, ma'am," I say, and down my coffee and rise to head for the door.

Abby says "wait," then ladles a cup of soup from a pot on the stove, moves over and hands it to me. She wraps her arms around my neck and whispers in my ear. "I hope I haven't been too forward. I fear we don't have time for a proper courtship."

"Abby, you just moving about this cabin was driving me crazy." Then I pause, and continue, "You know I'm a healthy man, or soon will be, and healthy men have needs—"

"You think I got that son by ignoring a man's needs?" She giggles, and pushes away from me.

I pause a moment and arrange the sweater so I can pull it on. And do so. "Fits fine," I say.

She smiles. "He'd be happy you have it, and you know something? I think you and I fit fine."

I feel the heat in my face, surprised I have any blush left in my old hide, and reach for the door, but she stops me with a hand on my arm.

"Linc, I want you to consider us packing up and riding out of here to the west, before a posse comes out of those woods across the meadow."

"Abby, you wouldn't want a man who didn't take care of business."

"Turn the other cheek, Linc."

"An eye for an eye, Abby."

She sighs deeply. "Then let's have what time we can together."

I nod, then say, "I'm going out to see if I can finish some of those saddle trees your man started."

Jed's voice rings out from the loft. "You want help, Linc?"

"It's Mister Dolan to you, young man," Abby yells back. "And you stop snooping."

"And it's Linc," I say, then turn to her, "with your permission, Abby."

She sighs again. "Fine. Is Twodogs back yet?"

"No, ma'am."

"It's Abby, not ma'am." Then she laughs and yells up to Jed. "Young Mister Quinn, you get down here and help Linc get to the barn."

"Help me in the barn if you'd like. I'm moving just fine."

"In the barn," she yells again, then walks back to bus the cups and kettle, shaking her head. "Men!" she says, then as an afterthought, turns back to us. "Jed, bring the half barrel into the cabin, please. I'm going to heat water for the barrel and put extra logs in the fireplace...warm it up in here. I'm having a bath in my room while I fix supper, then I expect you two to scrub the top layer off. And Mister Dolan, please leave the long Johns out so I can scrub them in the tub."

"It ain't Saturday, ma," Jed complains, hitting the bottom stair on this way to help me.

She winks at me, hands me Bama's coffee and cup of soup, and gives us both a smile. "Special occasion," she says. "And a bath never hurt a body. I'll yell when I'm ready to start supper and have some hot water for you two."

"What special occasion?" Jed asks, as we head to the barn.

I shrug, "Woman stuff," then add, "don't expect to ever understand the fair sex, young fella."

Jed returns the shrug, then pulls the barn door open.

Chapter Thirty One

IT WAS SUNDOWN BY THE TIME Dob returned to Helena from his task of putting up posters. He'd had to dismount and wait an hour in the cold as the crease on his side had opened and bled, but he eventually got it stopped. He knew Wentworth would have the office closed so he went straight to Paddy's Saloon and bellied up to the bar. He had been nursing a hangover all day and figured a little hair of the dog was just what he needed.

"Rosco, three fingers of Black Widow."

The fat bartender brought a glass and the bottle and poured it full, at least five fingers worth. "Fifteen cents, Dob." Then he gave the tall thin deputy a crooked grin. "You look like something the cat throwed up, Dob. So, I gave you a little extra. I heard you was riding after that Dolan fella and that damned no good black what killed Phinias and the Judge."

"I was, but my deputies, Tory and Bernie, got cold feet and run off. I couldn't go after them killers alone, so here I am. Besides, the snow up the mountain is already belly deep on the horses."

"Them no-accounts was both worthless as a beer what's nothing but foam. I ain't surprised they run off."

"Too much cold and snow for them, I'd guess."

Dob glanced back over his shoulder at a faro table, then snapped his gaze back to Rosco. Damn, it was the same drummer who'd been at Mattie's and then later in Wentworth's office.

Dob slammed the whiskey with one gulp, dropped a nickel and a dime on the bar, and started for the door when a voice rang out.

"Deputy. Dob was it?"

Half the heads in the bar turned so he couldn't merely continue out the door, so he stopped and turned back. The drummer was on his feet and moving his way.

"You yell at me?" Dob asked.

The man walked right up and, being a half head shorter than Dob, looked up quizzically. "You were over at Junket City last night, right?"

"Not me," Dob said with a shrug. "I was up the mountain huntin' killers. Why do you ask."

"By God you got a twin brother if that wasn't you."

"No brother, no Junket City."

"Okay, deputy. You say so. Did you hear about those fellows got themselves strung up?"

"Strung up?"

"Lynched, from the big tree in front of that closed up church."

"I did not. Any idea who the hell they were...or what they did?"

"Nope. I think the Marshal might have some idea about the who, and I told him the why. Ain't all that many red headed fellas ugly as that one got himself hung."

"Red head? I had a deputy who had red hair and went missing."

"You sure you weren't there last night. A woman got herself cut up and those two fellas got hung for the deed."

"I believe," Dob managed a snarl as he talked, "I'd know it if I was in Junket City, particularly if some fellas broke the law...me being a lawman and all."

The drummer held out both hands, palms out, in supplication. "Don't take offense deputy. Like I said, this fella looked like you."

"I got to make my rounds, just like I did last night."

Revenge of the Damned

"I thought you were up the mountain last night hunting killers?"

"Get back to your game, a'fore I find a reason for you to cool your heels in our jail."

The man shrugged, turned, and hurried back to his seat at the faro table.

Dob moved out the saloon door and crossed the dark road to lean against the front wall of the now closed barbershop. He reached inside his coat and pulled the makin's from his shirt pocket. Carefully rolling a cigarette, he watched through the windows of Paddy's. He wondered, would this drummer suddenly realize Dob, for sure, had been at Mattie's last night? Had he already convinced Wentworth that he was there? When and if Wentworth found out that his two drunken deputies had gotten themselves lynched over at Junket City, would Wentworth presume his deputy had been there too, and maybe knew some too much about that Belle woman getting sliced up?

Maybe, Dob thought, I should hightail it out of town?

Then again, maybe they'd bury Tory and Bernie as unknowns and nothing more would come of it. But, then again, lynching seldom went unnoticed, even though Montana was only a territory and a wild one at that.

Damn, it was all too much for Dob to think on. One thing he did know, if that damn drummer breathed his last this very night, he wouldn't be testifying to anything. Particularly anything to do with Dob's whereabouts last night.

Damn, damn, damn, he wished he wasn't so damn hung over. It would most likely affect his aim.

***

I enjoy my time in the barn, working on saddle trees with Jed, but to tell the truth am distracted. Am I being terribly selfish wanting to...to...get closer to Abby. I'm sure nothing could come of it but grief for her and the boy. I have, it seems, little or no future. I can't turn away from Maggie Mae's death. I might have had some chance of straightening things out if Judge Homer Stanley were still in office for it was rumored he was a fair man, but Bama had explained to me the fact Stanley had been shot dead. God only knows who's to replace him, and whoever it might be sure as hell would take Wentworth's word over mine. I have no future in Helena, probably in Montana, and nothing to offer Abby and Jed other than what protection I can provide, and with the law after me, that is likely of little value.

But when I respond to Abby's call, and Jed and I enter the cabin, all concern flies with the wind that is picking up outside. Abby wears a rose-colored dress that is rather daring at the neckline and trimmed in lace. Her hair is pulled back and she wears some silver on her ears and about her neck. When she points, without saying a word, at her bedroom and the tub I can see steaming just inside, and as I pass her, she smells of lilac. She is truly beautiful. All a man could ask for.

"Let's scrub," I say over my shoulder to the boy, and we enter the room closing the door behind. I reach deep into a pocket of my canvas trousers and bring out a coin. "You call it. Winner goes first."

"Loser you mean," Jed grouses.

"Call it," I say, and laugh when he wins.

Chapter Thirty Two

I AM UP BEFORE THE SUN, not quite sure if Jed and I are ready to confront each other quite so directly, as I tiptoe quietly out of Abby's bedroom. I can't get the smile off my face as I slowly close the door, perch on one of the ladder back chairs, pull my boots on, then feed the fire and move to the Buck stove and get it to going under the coffee pot. What a woman she is, I think, then get a twinge of guilt. As the water heats I walk to the window and see that Twodogs has returned from the hunt as his pinto is corralled.

I didn't beat Jed down by much, as by the time the coffee is perking the boy alights at the bottom of the stairway.

"How'd you and ma get on?" he asks, an impish grin covering his face.

I can't help but blush, a thing I'm doing more and more regular. "Just fine, thank you, young man. I'd let the subject rest when it comes to asking your mother, how-some-ever. Sometimes silence is the manly thing."

Jed laughs. "Okay, but how'd you and ma get on."

"Your mother is a beautiful and intelligent woman and I know you're proud to be her son...and, not that it's any of your business, but we got on just fine. I'm gonna cook up some hash with that leftover haunch, if you'll fetch me three or four of those big spuds out of the cellar."

"You bet," he says, and pulls the pie safe away from the opening, then disappears inside. As he does there is a quiet knock on the door. I limp over and check from the window. Twodogs.

I open the door and wave him in with some energy as it's snowing fairly heavily.

"How'd the hunt go?" I ask.

"Tell for coffee," the big Indian says, with as close to a smile as he ever gets.

"Should be ready," I reply, and pour three cups, adding two spoonfuls of sugar to both that of Twodog's and Jed's.

Twodogs nods, his way of thanking me.

"How'd it go?" I ask again.

"Slow, four grouse, kill with rocks."

"At least you saved some powder and they'll make a fine meal for the five of us. I'll bet Abby will roast them up tonight if you'll pluck and gut 'em."

Twodogs nodded. "Need more .44/.40, you got?"

"Only a handful. I got a gold piece if you want to go down the mountain."

"Junket maybe, no go Helena."

"Abby was saying she's low on sugar and flour and could use some dried apples. With luck this snow will quit."

"Have snowshoes. Will lead horse till can ride."

"I'll have Abby pack you some grub soon as she's up." I turn back and pour a crock full of coffee. "Jed will bring y'all out some breakfast in a bit. Share this with Bama," I say, and Twodogs nods.

"Hi, Twodogs," Jed says, as he pushes the pie safe back in place.

Twodogs gives the boy a nod and slips out the door.

***

Dob was fearful of going into the office. He'd hunkered down in the alley across from Beauregard's Bucket of Blood and waited, hoping he'd see the drummer leave and could follow him to some lonely spot and dispatch the som'bitch, but he'd fallen asleep and only awakened when the saloon's doors were shuttered and barred.

He'd shown no one the crease in his side as it would be hard to explain. So he had no excuse to beg off duty. When he walked in the office he was surprised to see Wentworth already at his desk.

"Get in here, Dob," the Marshal shouted at him.

So he stuck his head into the back office. "Yes, sir. You want coffee?"

"No, I want you to take a seat."

A shudder ran down Dob's back, but he moved on in and sat across from the big Marshal. "Sir?"

"Looks like the weather is clearing and I want you to ride over to Junket City and get some statements from folks regarding this lynching. Judge Horace J. Peabody, the new federal territorial judge, will be here this afternoon on the Huntley Stage, or so says the wire. And he's gonna want to know the status of everything we got on our plate. I got a hunch them two fellas that got lynched were your two runaways. You think that could be? If so, them fellas lynched a couple of lawmen, as flea bitten as they mighta been."

Dob shrugged. This was the worst possible news. Someone in Junket City would surely recognize him as having been there. Hell, that smart-alec black French whore he sliced up might even recognize him. And he had a crease on his side from her damned little belly gun. There wasn't no hiding that crease.

"Now, get me some coffee," Wentworth said, and continued with some paperwork on his desk.

At least the drummer hadn't given him up to the Marshal, maybe because he had enough doubt that he wasn't sure enough to do so. But Dob knew it was way too big a risk to return to Junket City, particularly this soon....

Nope, he'd have to buy some time, and get the hell out of town, and to be safe, out of the territory. The good news, the

Marshal had sent him out of town, and leaving on the town's dime with orders to go, would hardly be noticed.

He returned to the Marshal's desk and set the coffee down. "Marshal, I'll need to draw some traveling money, I'd better hire me a pack horse and tack as I don't want to get caught in a damn blizzard and just have some damn hardtack and jerky in a saddlebag. And it's only three days to payday. Could I draw my pay a'fore I go. I might not get back by then."

"You don't need no damn packhorse for a twelve mile trip."

"In this weather. Could get nasty out there."

"Looks to me like it's clearing."

Dob laughed nervously. "This is Montana, turn your head and turn it back and the weather done changed."

"I'm busy here, Dob. Get your ass over to hire you a mule to drag and three days vittles from Mayberry at the Merc. I'll have your damn pay when you get back here. Now leave me the hell alone. I got to get ready for this new judge."

"Peabody?"

"That's him. Go."

"Yes, sir," Dob said, and hurried out the door.

When he had the mule ready to pack, already loaded with two forty pound sacks of grain for the mule and his dappled gray, he headed over to Mayberry's and stomped in. "Forrest, I'm heading out on the hunt again and need to stock up."

"This on the city, Dob?" Mayberry asked.

"It is. A couple of weeks' grub, cartridges, and a new Winchester...Henry model if you got one."

"You're talking twenty, twenty-five dollars, Dob. You got some kind of authorization?"

Dob stared at Forrest Mayberry as if he had a boil on the end of his nose. "Damn, Forrest, how long have I been coming in this store of yours. How many times have I insisted the Marshal's office keep trading with you, even if Wentworth wanted to go out to Smith's and buy from—"

"Wentworth wanted to trade with Smith?"

"He did, but I fought hard for you as you always been fair—"

"I got a near new '66,' .44/.40 center fire carbine length, good for a saddle boot. She's as pretty as a speckled pup. I bet you'll like her."

"That was just what I had in mind. And four boxes of cartridges for it and two of .45s for my Scofield. I'll pick out my necessities while you get her down."

"My pleasure, Dob," the merchant said, and fetched a stool to get the new lever action down. "Damn, six boxes, you must be after a flock of killers."

"I am, Forrest, I sure am," Dob said, as he headed for a handful of good cigars. Since this would be the last time he'd see Helena, he might as well do it up right.

Chapter Thirty Three

DOB RODE OUT OF HELENA well before noon with forty-seven dollars in his pocket, dragging a mule with nearly a month's worth of grub and enough ammunition for his new Winchester for half a year of hunting and two boxes of .45s for his top-break Smith and Wesson. He only rode a mile northwest, then cut back to pick up the Mullan Road and up the mountain. East toward the river would be easier, but more likely to run into someone who'd recognize him, and that's the way anyone would think a fella on the run would go. Towards the river, which was still a long way from freezing up. No one would figure a fella would take on the mountain with the snow already belly deep up on top the pass. So that was the way he'd go.

Dob had been around Montana long enough to know these early snows might look like things were going to close in, then hell, they may melt off completely before the real winter took over and made travel damn near impossible. Nope it was over the pass. The stage wouldn't try the pass and would be turning around and heading back to Fort Benton, because of the weather. He should have the road all to himself.

So, it was over the mountain. Wentworth would likely send somebody looking for him when he didn't return, but they'd head for Junket City, and he'd be over the pass and headed toward Deer Lodge and maybe half way to Missoula before they knew he was missing, or until Mayberry reported the amount of supplies he'd loaded up along with the rifle he wasn't authorized to procure. Until then they'd likely think him killed by some of those no accounts in Junket City or them murderers what was running free.

Dob laughed when he thought of Wentworth, and how beet red in the face he'd be when he learned his deputy had lit a shuck and left him with a twenty seven dollar and forty cent tab at Mayberry's. And Bartleston at the livery where he'd hired the mule would surely go after the city for the cost of the mule and tack he dragged behind. Wentworth would likely have apoplexy.

But as he climbed Mullan Road toward the pass, he began to wonder if he hadn't bit off more than he could chew. The snow was deep and the wind began to howl and it would soon be deeper.

***

Wentworth, his books and records in order, if mostly a well-constructed lie, stood, hat in hand, while the Huntley Stage and its six-up, throwing mud and slush behind, made its way up to the stage station. The Marshal was accompanied by Delbert O'Brien a miner and city councilman, Howard Polkinghorn also a miner and city councilman, Wilfred McAllister the station master at Huntley's, and Tiny Allendorf who ran the Cattlemen's Saloon and Hotel. The governor, Benjamin F. Potts, would have been there, but he was in far off Washington D.C. It seemed he often made an excuse to travel to the capitol and his ancestral home in Ohio during the Montana winters.

Peabody was a tall man, stately, and wore a stovepipe hat reminiscent of Lincoln. He had been a general in the Union Army during the war and served with distinction, if only as a legal attaché to the headquarters in Washington. It was rumored he had his eyes set on a territorial governorship, possibly Montana's.

He dismounted from the Concord and brushed himself off then shook hands with the contingency there to greet him.

He eyed Wentworth carefully as he'd known him during the war, and was less than favorably inclined towards him…but was polite.

"Would you be ready for a drink, Judge," Wentworth asked. "On us, of course," he added.

"It's my habit, Marshal, to pay my own way, but I'll be happy to wet my dry, dusty throat with you gentlemen, after I find myself an abode and get some of this God forsaken cold out of my bones. Is this temperature normal this early?"

"No sir, it's an abomination, but it'll pass before the real winter sets in."

"I hope so. Did you arrange some accommodations until I have a chance to find a permanent home?"

"Cattlemen's, the presidential suite, if that suits you. The best room in the territory."

"It'll do for tonight, but then I'll take some more frugal space."

"As you wish." The city councilmen each grabbed one of the Judge's four bags, as the coachman and hostler pulled a steamer trunk from the Concord's boot.

"You'll deliver that to the Cattlemen's," Wentworth snapped at the pair.

"Please," Peabody said to the men, then gave Wentworth a derisive glance. "You haven't mellowed much, have you Oscar?"

"Mellow don't keep a town like Helena honest, Judge," Wentworth replied.

"Humph," Peabody said, then demurred to the men. "Lead the way, gentlemen."

***

When the snow got more than knee deep on Dob's dappled gray, the mule began to take umbrage and sat back, nearly dragging Dob from the saddle. The snow had just stopped

Revenge of the Damned

falling and he was gaining confidence that he'd make the pass by nightfall tomorrow.

As the sun finally came out, but was only a half hour from touching the mountain top ahead of him, he decided to find a place to camp and searched the fir stand to his right as he plodded up the mountain, until he saw a thick stand with nearly snowless ground beneath its heavy branches.

Smiling to himself he reined the animals up the slight incline...when a snowshoe rabbit broke from only a foot beneath his horse, and the animal reared, somersaulting Dob over backwards...and he kicked the mule on the nose on his way to landing flat on his face with an oomph that echoed down the canyon.

The mule, too, went up on its hind legs, scattering goods from its panniers and landing hard with a hoof on the back of Dob's knee. The deputy's scream quickly followed his oomph, and the mule humpbacked away down the mountain, shedding himself of the rest of his load, throwing bundles and camping utensils in every direction.

To add insult to injury, his horse followed, taking the new Winchester and Scofield and gun belt that was hanging on the saddlehorn.

Dob tried to climb quickly to his feet to chase after the animals, but his badly bruised knee gave out and he went to his face in the snow.

As he watched his animals, now two hundred or more yards down the mountain, continue to disappear, his curses rang after his oomph and cries.

"Damn, damn, damn," he moaned, then settled and took stock of his situation. His foodstuffs and other supplies were spread all over the mountain, but at least he had them. He had a flint and steel in his pocket, thank God, and could build a fire. If he'd have had half a brain he'd have kept his Scofield strapped on his hip.

Tomorrow, his knee willing, he'd gather as much grub as he could carry and start down the mountain. But he couldn't go back to Helena.

Wentworth would be mad as a hornet and would likely jail him, or worse, so it had to be Junket City...and Junket was closer anyhow.

Right now it was grab what chow he could, and find a dry spot and some firewood.

He whined again as he shoved himself upright and his knee shouted at him to stay off it...but he couldn't.

Chapter Thirty Four

TERRITORIAL JUDGE HORACE Jasper Peabody was scowling so deeply it looked as if his face had been plowed. He sucked on a cigar and blew smoke, not casually in rings, but in blasts.

They were seated at a round table in a rear corner of the Cattlemen's, fat steaks on platter sized plates surrounded by fried potatoes and green beans cooked with thick sliced bacon. Thick hard crusted bread was slathered with butter. Mugs of beer flanked the platters.

The judge exhaled a billow of smoke, then cleared his throat and demanded, "Marshal, tell me again who you've got coming to help you enforce the law here? I hope I didn't hear you correctly."

"Not enforce the law here, Judge, but to go on the trail and bring back the murderer Dolan and Judge Stanley's killer. If you was to be shot down I'm sure you'd want me to hire the best—"

"Best? Best damn killers in the territory, you mean?"

"Best trackers, best law-dogs, besides yours truly, of course."

"Wentworth, when I was in Bismarck I was a breath away from putting warrants out for the Tollofsons, Guzman, and that McCallester fella. They are not the kind of men you want here in Helena."

"They won't be staying after they finish their task."

Peabody shook his head with some obvious disgust. "You know the stories going 'round about the four of them. A dozen crimes, but no witnesses, at least no live ones. Rape, murder and enough robbery to be yielding a pile big enough to build you a new jail...and they damn sure should be in one. They shot and hung over twenty of the Brooksbury gang. Some thought it was law enforcement. I think it was culling out the competition."

Wentworth took a moment, then cleared his throat, "Judge, you know there's stories to fill a book about any of us who have to bang heads, and worse, to clean up some railhead town or mining burg which at times requires scatterguns and six shooters. I'll bet there's an encyclopedia full about me and I wouldn't be surprised, with the enemies a judge garners in his honest work, that there would be a list long as my arm about you."

That made Peabody chuckle, and Wentworth felt relieved as he was pushing it a mite.

The judge knocked the ash off his cigar into a spittoon next to his chair then got serious again. "I'll say no more about it, Marshal. But you mark my words, you've invited four wolves into the lamb pen."

"I can handle them, Judge. I can," Wentworth said, but even he seemed to doubt it.

***

Morning crept in quietly, with the sun starting a melt and the moon having taken all the clouds with her.

Twodogs had not ridden out to Junket City when night fell, as the snowfall had worsened, but when Abby peeked out the window at the break of dawn she was pleased to see him saddling up his pinto. She had just spooned the last of the coffee into the big porcelain pot and after mixing batter for a platter full of biscuits, would only have enough flour for a cake or another load of biscuits.

Revenge of the Damned

The hens had quit laying with the cold weather, so it was biscuits, beans, and side pork for breakfast. She went to the door and yelled out, "Mister Twodogs, I have breakfast on the stove and a list for you...presuming you're going to Junket City?"

"Will the store there take any saddle trees?" I yell from Abby's room.

"They took two finished pack saddles last year and would likely take another."

"None finished yet," I say, stepping out of her room, yawning and stretching widely. "Woman, you'd ruin a man. I haven't slept this late since the war and that after one of those three day forced marches."

"Coffee is ready. Take a seat and I'll pour. And, sir, if you consider what we do as ruination, we can always stop the doing of it?"

I laugh. "No, ma'am. I'm proud to be ruined."

"Thought so," she says, giving me a knowing smile.

I move to the table, stopping in some wonderment as I realize I'm not limping to get there. "Dang if I'm not feeling pretty darn fit. I believe we could go dancing."

"Come spring, we'll dance in Oregon or Washington," she says, and I know she's serious.

I say, with no pleasure, "After my chores in Helena."

She ignores my reply. "What would you like on your biscuits, Mister Dolan?"

"A couple of fried eggs, but since we don't have—"

"We have honey, apple butter, or some sorghum. What will it be?"

"Apple butter, that'll be my choice."

"Linc," she says, opening the oven and checking on her two tins of biscuits.

"Ma'am?"

She turns to me and shakes a finger. "Don't you start thinking you can jump up and start chopping wood. We have plenty of help—"

"I just said I was feeling good. I won't go picking any fights with grizzly bears...at least for a while."

"Linc, please stop talking about that...that Helena affair. I'm sure you think you have to do something, but I don't want to hear about it. It makes me very sad."

I'm quiet a moment, then rise and skirt the table and wrap my arms around her and give her a hug and whisper in her ear. "The last thing I want to do is make you unhappy. In fact, when I finish—"

"Don't. Don't talk about it," she says, and pushes me away.

I stand for a moment, then move back to my seat. "Apple butter, if you don't mind." It's the closest thing to trading cross words we've had since I arrived.

Jed comes down the stairs three at a time, then stops short. "What? What's the matter?"

"Not a thing," I say, giving the boy a wide grin. "Sun is up and shining bright, I'm feeling fit as a fiddle, and you're up and already run a comb through that tangle of your'n. And the best of all, your ma has a platter full of biscuits on the way."

"Something was botherin' you two."

"Your ma was just giving me a lecture on not puttin' a strain on it yet, that's all."

"Good. Ma, can I ride in with Twodogs, should he be going today?"

"No, young man. You can gather us some firewood and look in on Bama from time to time. With Twodogs gone and these other two stove up, I need a healthy man about."

"But—"

"No buts. Now go wash your hands. I poured the bowl full of hot water not a half hour ago."

"Yes, ma'am," Jed mumbles, but he isn't happy about not being able to ride into town.

"Is Twodogs going?" I ask.

"He's going," Abby replies.

"I'll give him a penny for a couple of jaw-beakers," I say, and wink at Jed.

"Peppermint, tell him."

"You tell him," Abby says. "Go fetch him for breakfast, and help Mister Bama in. I'd like us all to say grace and eat together."

"Yes, 'um," Jed says, and runs for the door.

Chapter Thirty Five

DOB SLEPT FITFULLY UNDER the heavy boughs of a fir. The crease in his side was worrying him, it had healed over, but was red and swollen. The fire he'd managed to get going had to be kept low, or the tree itself might catch fire, and even low it mostly served to melt the snow above. He didn't have to sleep in the snow but he did sleep under a weeping cover of snow topped branches. His coat was heavy wool, and shed the water fairly well, but his canvas pants were beginning to soak through.

When he tried to get out from under the boughs he discovered his knee was swollen to twice its size and wouldn't hold his weight. So, he crawled through the snow to collect what foodstuffs he could, cussing the weather as it had topped everything with three inches of snow and much of what he'd seen after the damn critters ran off was hidden—covered in white. Even though it was sunny, he couldn't find much of which the mule had gotten shed. He did find the two sacks of grain and a side of bacon, and a small cast iron skillet. He crawled, dragging what he could find back under the tree. He was able to melt water in the skillet, then fry up some bacon.

He filled his stomach, then lay back, and wondered if he was going to die under this damn weeping tree.

***

Revenge of the Damned

Marie Bellerose, the French mulatto from Mattie's, had been relegated to a very small room behind the kitchen. She no longer would draw the men with the most gold in their pocket, so she lost the prime location in the house. The gash from ear to jaw on the left side of her face was stitched together by Mattie herself, but was swollen and angry making her face unbalanced and hard to look upon.

Luckily, she had over four hundred dollars hidden under a floorboard in her former room. Now, God willing, no one would discover it until she could get it back. Mattie had assured her she could return to work as a pleasure lady as soon as she healed, but likely never back in the spacious room she'd occupied as Mattie's pride and joy, and top earner by nearly four times.

Until healed, Maddie agreed to put her to work in the kitchen for a dollar a day and food. But deep in Belle's heart she hoped she'd never have to return to the life of a whore. She wanted to take her hidden money and head west. She had enough to start her own restaurant, and it would be only that, a restaurant. She knew she was lucky not to have taken the pox from her former line of work, and that if she'd continued, her luck would've eventually run out. She'd been blessed; blessed not to have been killed by the crazy man in the fur coat, blessed not to have gotten the pox, blessed to have had her beauty for as long as she had.

She'd bide her time, get her hands back on her stash and hide it somewhere closer, and come spring she'd catch the stage south to Cheyenne and then the transcontinental all the way west to San Francisco.

She'd work the kitchen in her own Cajun style restaurant. No one cared if the cook was ugly, so long as the food was good.

***

Twodogs started out for Junket City with his saddle bags full of hard tack and jerky, dragging Abby's palomino as a pack horse. He liked jerky, but more to his liking was the four biscuits Abby had stuffed into the bags, two slathered with apple butter and two with a half-inch thick layer of bacon. It would only take him a little over half a day to reach the little mining town—now rapidly becoming a ghost town—should the snow depth lessen as he got nearer the road the white eyes called Mullan.

He'd depend on his snowshoes, made of bent willow and rawhide, in the deep snow, while leading his pinto with the palomino tied behind.

After trudging through the snow, dragging the animals who had to hump from time to time, Twodogs spotted the road a couple of hundred feet below. He was able to mount when he reached it, but didn't. He kicked the snow off a blowdown fir and plopped down to let the horses blow and to catch a breath himself.

Then he decided it was a good time, on a comfortable perch with the sun beating down, to fill his belly with a biscuit or two. He dug into his saddle bags, then stopped suddenly. Looking over the horses backs he saw a man, afoot, a hundred paces on down the mountain in the shadows of a copse of pine, staring at him.

So rather than pause to eat, he mounted, drawing his Winchester from its elk-hide saddle boot and laying it across his thighs, and gigged his horse forward. The pinto sensed where he was headed, its ears tilted forward, its eyes never straying from the man. The snow was now only a foot deep, and easy going for the horses.

When Twodogs was only forty paces away, the man, who had slipped behind a pine, carefully limped away from the tree trunk into the open. He cupped his hands on his mouth, and yelled, "Twodogs. Damn you are a sight for sore eyes."

Twodogs kept moving forward, eyeing the deputy, smiling inwardly as he could see that Dob was not armed. And he was a man on Twodogs' list, a man he meant to kill, and the great spirit had served him up.

It was too good to be true.

And the man seemed to be wounded. He could barely move, lifting one leg with a hand in back, as he moved out of the copse of trees onto the road. He was smiling stupidly.

Even though he knew he should just shoot the deputy who'd left him to die on the road along with Wentworth, he was curious what brought the man to be unarmed and seemingly horseless so far from town.

"What want?" he asked when he got only a few feet from the man.

"Well, goddang man, can't you see I'm hurt and afoot."

"Not my problem." Twodogs searched the trees up and down the road, thinking it might be some kind of trap. Maybe they knew he'd killed the barber?

"Why, man, what do you mean. I could die out here."

"Why you here?"

Dob was silent a moment, then decided to level with the Indian. He knew the Indian had no love lost for Wentworth, so he told a small lie. "I had me a falling out with Marshal Wentworth. He went to sassing me so I whipped him bad. Broke his fat nose and maybe knocked out some teeth. He called in a bunch of lowlifes so I had to run for it." He eyed Twodogs carefully, wondering if he was convincing him, then doubting it, continued, "And they's a new judge, Horace Peabody, and he don't like me none. If'n I go back they'll put me in the hoosegow."

"Hoosegow?" Twodogs asked.

"Jail, the gol'dang jailhouse."

Twodogs shrugged. "Why I not kill you?"

"Kill me?" Dob stumbled back a couple of steps. "Hell's fire, man, I never done nothing to you. I'll tell you something, they got a poster out on you. You're a wanted man. You, that nigra…maybe you don't know about him…and that Dolan we was all hunting. You ain't seen them other fellas have you?

We could make a lot of money, we take them in…I can't, but you can."

"How much money?" Twodogs asked.

"Five hundred each. That's a thousand dollars, Twodogs. But I got to heal up some first."

Chapter Thirty Six

DOB WAS TALKING AS FAST as he could, worrying the big Indian was about to use the Winchester on him. He had no intention of partnering up with Twodogs, but if he could get a horse and stay with the Crow until they bedded down somewhere, he could get his hands on that Winchester, then he'd have a horse, in fact two horses and tack, and the money he was planning to offer for the packhorse back.

"Twodogs, I can buy that packhorse, you wanna sell him. I'll give you twenty dollars in gold."

That sealed it for Twodogs, a man he hated, a man he wanted to kill no matter, but even though he did not have a horse or a gun as a prize, he had at least twenty dollars in gold.

"Twenty not enough," Twodogs said.

"Okay, twenty-five, gold coin."

"Thirty," Twodogs countered.

"Damn, you part Jew tinker, or what? Okay, okay, thirty dollars."

"Let me see coin." Twodogs wanted to make sure he had the money on him, not buried somewhere.

Dob dug in a pocket and came up with four ten-dollar gold pieces. He quickly returned one to his pocket. "Let's trade," he said with a cockeyed grin, then added, "I'll throw in another ten, you want to sell that fancy Indian saddle?"

"No sell saddle."

Dob shrugged. "Okay, hand over that pack horse and you can have three of these ten dollar gold pieces."

"Price now forty dollars," Twodogs said, tight lipped, as close to a smile as he ever got.

"No, by God, you saw that other coin but you ain't getting it. We done made a deal." But he knew it didn't matter as he'd kill the Indian first chance he had and get back whatever he paid.

"You want bet?" Twodogs asked.

"Bet, bet what?"

"Bet I get forty," with that he swung the muzzle of his Winchester, leveling it on Dob's chest, and cocking it.

To Dob, the ratcheting of the hammer sounded like a steam train bearing down with him tied to the tracks.

He spoke even faster. "Hell man, you can have all forty dollars. I'm already shot." He pulled his coat aside and shirt up, showing the graze on his side. "Just let me ride along. I'll help you do whatever. I'll help you catch them other fellas. It's a thousand dollars you catch that Bama and Dolan, or five hundred you catch even one. Man could live real good in Crow country with even five hundred dollars. Buy himself a dozen squaws or fifty horses—"

Twodogs held his hand out, palm facing Dob. "No talk. I know where Dolan and Bama. You ride with me. We will go there."

Dob exhaled a long deep breath. "Okay. All right. You let me ride that horse. You give me that side arm, we'll go get them murderers and make us a pile of gold."

"Us?"

"Okay, you. But I got to ride. My knee done been stomped by a mule, and my shank's mare ain't working so good?"

"Shank's mare?" Twodogs asked.

"I ain't walking so good."

"Got to go Junket City for supplies—"

"I can't go there. I surely can't."

"Got to go Junket City for supplies. You hide in woods. After, we go Dolan. We go Bama."

153

Revenge of the Damned

Dob chewed on that a moment, then nodded slowly. "I can lay low in the woods, then we go?"

Twodogs nodded, then walked back to his pinto and the palomino, and led the pack horse back to Dob.

"You got to help me mount?" Dob said.

"Log help," Twodogs said, and pointed to a blowdown fir.

Dob obliged, hoisting himself up onto the uncomfortable, stirrup-less pack saddle, and, with Dob leading, they set off toward Junket City.

***

Marshal Oscar Wentworth had spent a good part of the morning composing a wire to send to Guzman via the Marshal in Bozeman, calling him off from coming. He didn't enjoy the wrath of the judge for his choice of helpers, yet the more he thought on it didn't want to deal with four killers, or at least four reputed to be killers. He'd gotten posters out on Dolan, the nigra, and the Indian and that would do for the time being. The hell of it was, he gave little thought to the nigra and the Indian, but Dolan was another matter. The Irishman had shamed him, and every time he saw a couple of fellas yapping and they glanced over at him, then guffawed or even smiled coyly, he was positive they were discussing the fact his wife, Maggie Mae, had tripped up that fine carpeted stairway at the Cattlemen's and disappeared into another man's room.

No, Dolan was another thing altogether, and he would have the Irishman's hide tacked to the outhouse wall, so he could tear off a piece when needed for butt wipe.

The telegraph office would have normally been located in or very near the railroad station, but since Helena wasn't blessed with a railroad, was a room in Huntley's.

As he neared Huntley's, McAllester, the station master strode out the door. "Oscar, you saved me a walk."

"How so?" Wentworth asked.

"Got a wire from the stage station in Three Forks. Those fellas you hired will be here tomorrow, the weather don't keep them sheltered up somewheres along the way."

"Guzman?" Wentworth couldn't help but ask.

"Guzman and three more."

"Damn," Wentworth mumbled.

"Why damn? I thought you wanted some help?"

Wentworth wadded up the paper with the message he'd composed and stuffed it in his pocket. "Sure did. You going to lunch, Will? It's been a month of Sundays since you bought the town Marshal lunch."

Willfred McAllester eyed the Marshal, but bit his tongue. "I was going to skip lunch, but sure, I'll buy."

"I hear Beauregard's got a whole mess of fresh trout in. Let's head up the gulch."

"My pleasure," McAllester lied.

Damn, Wentworth thought as the headed for Beauregard's Bucket of Blood, I sure as hell hope the weather clears up and this snow melts off. I'm not looking forward to having them four owlhoots stuck in town for a good long time. They ain't the kind to stay out of trouble, and I ain't a bit interested in going up against four infamous shootists.

Chapter Thirty Seven

MARIE 'BELLE' BELLEROSE took her bandage off for the first time, and stood staring into the mirror in the room that served as the pleasure ladies' waiting room, lounge, and occasionally an area for private entertainment for the gentlemen. At the moment she had it all to herself. And she was glad she did as she broke down in tears, sobbing at the sight of the long scar. Sadie Mississippi was now ensconced in her old room, and when she saw Sadie entertaining a rich miner and enjoying a steak and whiskey with him, Belle had slipped up the back stairs with a pry-bar and recovered her money. She hadn't been able to get the floor board properly back in place, and hoped Sadie or her customer didn't trip and break something.

Counting her savings she was surprised to discover it was even more than she'd thought. Five hundred and twenty-seven dollars in gold. Mostly in five-dollar gold pieces as she'd often received four dollars for her service and a dollar tip.

However, as she studied the ugly scar, she wondered if she'd earn a dollar a poke from now on...if there was a now on.

She spent half the night sewing gold pieces into the lining of a thick wool coat she had, and under the flap of its fur collar. The coat was now pounds heavier, but she was sure no one would notice. With winter bearing down, heavy coats would be the order of the day.

As she was walking out of the lounge, she ran into Barney in the hall. "You oughta keep that ugly thing covered," he snapped.

"Oh, you think the dishes gonna be offended? I be in the kitchen, not out among the customers."

"Don't get smart with me, Belle. You ain't the belle of the ball no more."

"Nice of y'all to mention it, Mister Barney," she said, her lip quivering.

"Just shut the hell up, Belle. I did you a good turn hanging those no accounts what cut you up."

"If they was the ones?"

"What the hell do you mean, if they was the ones?"

"You didn't ask me nothing. You just hung 'em up like slabs of side pork and I saw you and you was enjoying it."

"There ain't no if about it, you bitch. I saw that coat running away on the back of the fella that sliced you—"

"But the fella sliced me was tall and skinny and didn't have a beard, and the fellas you hung...one was short and one had a beard that would shame Methuselah."

"Who the hell is Methuselah? Don't matter. You don't be doubtin' who we hung to nobody else, you understand."

"I understand, but it wasn't the son of a bitch that cut me."

Barney snaked a heavy hand out and grabbed Belle by the throat and shoved her up against the wall. "Look, you bitch, you ain't worth a skunk's whiff so you do exactly what I say. You say the fella we hung was the fella that sliced you, understand?"

Belle tried to nod, but couldn't with Barney's corn cob fingers throttling her slender neck. But he let her go before she passed out, and she sunk to both knees.

"You understand?" he snapped again.

"Yes...yes, sir," she managed.

"I'll be coming to your crib tonight, after Mattie starts to snoring, and you won't say nothing about that, you understand that?"

"Yes, yes, nothing," she managed.

He spun on his heel and headed back to the front of the saloon, and she lay there, coughing, trying to catch a breath, and watched him go.

She hoped he didn't come. She'd heard from the other girls what a rough, mean, son of a bitch he was, doing things he wouldn't allow customers to do to the girls.

He'd always left her alone, as she was the prize of the place and earned both he and Mattie four times what any other girl earned, even Sadie who now had her room.

Hope wasn't the word for it, she prayed he didn't come.

***

Jed and I have been working hard in the barn, and now have Bama's help. If he moves wrong Bama takes a few deep gasps and grabs his side, his cuts are healing nicely but his ribs will take a while longer to mend, even as tough as Bama is.

But he is handy as can be, and can use a file and shape the pieces of the saddle trees to what seems a hundredth of an inch, so they fit perfectly. And then I drill and peg, and Jed glues. Then they're clamped to dry. Well, we make a fine team of shapers and fitters.

We have a dozen and a half saddle trees drying and are now working on a half dozen pack saddles, as Abby says they've sold well also.

Abby, who I'm beginning to not only lust after, but to love, occupies half of my thinking time. I'm getting way too settled into this little cabin and its barn and pasture, and am beginning to believe that settling my and Maggie Mae's debt might not be as important as I'd thought. I owe Maggie Mae, but every day I owe Abby more, and every day I feel closer to her and the boy.

And I know Abby's right, we can't stay on this mountain, so close to Helena, too close to Wentworth. We have too head out for Oregon or Washington. But can I live with myself if I let Maggie Mae's killer, craven cowardly killer that he is, get away with her murder? I fear it will haunt me the rest of my days if I don't avenge her death.

I think we've been very lucky to last this long without the Marshal and a posse of a dozen men riding down on us. Normally a woman and boy would be ignored, not taken to task for letting a wanted man hide out among them…but now there are two other wanted men on the place. Hell, in the eyes' of the law, in the eyes' of the people of Helena, Abby's place would be a nest of vipers.

And Abby and the boy could end up at the mercy of Marshal Oscar Wentworth, who's already killed a woman in cold blood.

I take a deep breath and then and there decide risking Abby and the boy to Wentworth's wrath is not worth me hanging around to get my satisfaction. We'll move on with the first thaw.

I've noticed that Mister Quinn has what the boy calls a bone pile. Quinn had salvaged a number of wrecked wagons to use the wood, Hickory from the east, Mahogany and Teak from the west, to build his saddle trees and pack saddles, and in that bone pile are a half dozen wagon wheels and at least four of them are in good shape. So, I decide to turn my talents, as limited as they might be, to building a wagon to haul us out of here to the west, come the snow melt.

To my pleasant surprise as we begin the work on the wagon, I discover that Bama is a skilled wagon builder. He's quickly assembled the undercarriage and fitted the axles, hubs, and wheels as fine as Mister Studebaker might have done.

It would forever be caught in my craw if I don't avenge Maggie Mae, but not so much as if I get Abby and Jed caught up in my troubles, or worse.

Hell, I have all winter, with snow already four feet deep in the canyon and ravine bottoms, no one will be coming up the mountain until spring.

At least I pray not.

Chapter Thirty Eight

WENTWORTH WAS SURPRISED when a fella a half head shorter than himself but equally wide-chested pushed into his office at midmorning. The man wore two revolvers, butt forward for cross draws, and had bandoliers, each with at least two dozen cartridges, crossing his chest. He wore the flat brimmed hat of a Texas vaquero, but spoke with little or no accent.

"You Wentworth?" he asked, crossing through the empty outer office and into the Marshal's without the bother of a knock.

"It's customary to knock," Wentworth said, but sounded way less offended than he meant to.

"I guess you'd have your door shut you wanted privacy," the man growled in return. "I'm Guzman, my associates are headed to a saloon to get a drink...said they'd stop at the first one they came to, and that would be?"

"That would be Cattlemen's, under the three story hotel of the same name. I was about to send you a wire when I got the one saying you'd be here today. We got heavy snow...impossible to get over the pass or into the high country. I won't be needing y'all till come spring thaw."

"Don't make a hoot nor a holler to me, Wentworth...but we come as requested so you owe me and my boys a month's wages. And I saw some posters on the way in. This Dolan fella, and this black, Bama I think it said...that five hundred a piece still good?"

Wentworth was a little red in the face. "A month? It didn't take you no month to get here—"

"A month. We turned down other work," Guzman scowled at him, crossing his arms across his belly, each hand too close to a gun butt for comfort.

Wentworth shrugged a little sheepishly. "You can't do your job, you can't get to the high country or over the pass."

"Come on outside, Wentworth," Guzman said, and headed for the front door.

Wentworth hesitated a minute, wondering if the man wanted him outside to shoot him full of holes, but he gulped, took a deep breath, and followed.

Guzman was waiting in the front doorway, making sure he was following.

They stepped out and Guzman asked, "See them?"

"Them what?"

"Them Percherons...you blind?"

"Those two tied to the rail?"

"You see any other Percherons about?"

Again, Wentworth shrugged.

Guzman continued, "That black weighs a ton, the gray slightly more. That wagon over there has saddles and bags twice the size of the usual. You aim old Caesar and Octavius up the mountain and they'll go till the snow's more'n belly deep. A little snow won't be holding us back. So what is it, Wentworth? You gonna pay up for the trouble of getting here as you requested or are we going to work catching them outlaws?"

Wentworth cleared his throat, then said, but unconvincingly, "You'll be working for wages. Them rewards is for folks other than the law."

Guzman laughed. "Sure, you pay us and we'll quit about five minutes before we run them to ground."

Wentworth frowned, but just shook his head.

"We'll take our pay, and the reward."

"You'll kick back half as it was me got you the work."

Revenge of the Damned

Guzman laughed again, but not in the eyes, there he was scowling. "I'll tell you what, lawman, we'll throw you in for a tenth…that'd be one hundred."

"There's four of you, right."

"You count pretty good."

"So, equal shares. Two hundred each."

It was Guzman's turn to shrug, then he added, "We'll take a month wages in advance, and you'll get your two hundred share of the reward."

Wentworth nodded. It would be hard to explain to the city council why he paid in advance, but better than having four very angry, and proven bad, hombres wanting a piece of his hide. And, after all, they'd come all the way from Bozeman in this lousy weather.

"When you going to ride out?" Wentworth asked, not wanting them to hang around Helena any longer than absolutely necessary.

"Sun up will work. The four of us and a guide, you'll provide, we'll ride until the smaller horses can't make it, then McCallester and I will get on them big fellas there. You got any idea where these two were headed?"

"They headed west, and if I know my country, they're up there on the mountain somewhere as getting over the pass has been nigh to impossible, but I'll tell you about it at supper."

"Kind of you to invite us," Guzman said with a laugh.

Wentworth gulped, then figured he'd take them to O'Dells, where he could fill them up on Irish stew and bad beer, then he remembered, "Damn, I forgot…we got a new territorial judge—"

"Peabody…I know the son of a bitch."

"Well, sir, Judge Peabody want's to have supper with y'all. I imagine too make sure the four of you mind your manners and abide by the law in Montana Territory."

Guzman gave him a crooked smile. "I guess I can put up with his palaver so long as it's over a thick steak."

There goes my cheap supper bill, Wentworth thought, but merely sighed.

"What time, and where?" Guzman asked.

"How about six thirty at Cattlemen's? That's likely where your boys are now."

"Okay. Now, where's the best looking covey of quail in town?"

"Quail?" Wentworth asked.

"How about tail. The best-looking tail. My boys will be wanting to get some of the poison out of their system…and to spend a little of that advance you're about to provide. Shall we walk over to the bank, or do you carry that kind of cash in your safe?"

If I did, I wouldn't tell you, Wentworth thought, then started across the street and waved Guzman to follow. "No cash in the office. Come on. Two blocks to the Miner's and Merchant's."

"I noticed a livery that a'way. Let's lead these two big fellas. I want them to grain up and get full of piss and vinegar if they're a gonna climb tomorrow."

Chapter Thirty Nine

DOB RODE AHEAD OF TWODOGS all the way to a thick copse of lodge pole pine a quarter mile from Junket City, where he reined up and turned to look over his shoulder. "Twodogs, I think this is close enough. I'll hide out here till you fill your list. You give a yell when you come back this way." Then he reined toward the trees.

"Down from horse," Twodogs commanded.

"What?"

"Down from horse. I take horse in."

Dob shrugged. Of course the Indian had to take the pack horse in. He'd hoped he'd get away by keeping him back, then riding the hell away, but it wasn't to be. Besides, there was a chance, a slight chance but a chance, that the Indian actually knew where Dolan and the black were hiding out, and if he did and Dob could bring them both in dead over a horse, even Wentworth would…might…forgive him his recent sins.

The store in Junket City was little more than four log walls and a canvas top, but it had everything on Twodogs' list.

His work was done, but he was in no hurry. It was beginning to get dark. It didn't much matter when he left out, it would be well past midnight by the time they got back.

So, why not have a drink of whiskey or two…if the bartender in Maddie's would serve him. He had been refused service in other saloons who would not serve Indians.

He wandered down the road, leading his pinto and the pack horse and tied them at the rail where a half dozen horses were already hitched.

***

Maddie had taken ill that morning, something that made her stomach roil and had caused her to half fill the pail Barney had placed by her bed.

One thing was sure to Barney, she wouldn't be crawling out of her bed until tomorrow at least.

Since she hadn't been there to badger him, he'd been working the bottle pretty hard all day. There were only a half dozen miners in the place. Gilda, the cook, could handle any food or serving that needed doing, and his swamper, Henry Jennings, would consider it an honor to be trusted to take over the bar for a while. Henry was a small man, sometimes called 'Mouse' by Maddie, but she called him that good-naturedly.

So, needing someone to fill in, Barney called him over. "Henry, I'll be going up to see to Maddie. You pour an honest drink, and don't get sticky fingers...put what goes in the till in the till."

"Yes, sir," Henry said with a toothless grin.

"I catch you robbin' us and I'll pull one of your arms off'n you and use it to beat you to death, you understand?"

"Yes, sir. I'm honest as a sunny Sunday morning."

"I don't know why Sunday might be any more honest than any other day—"

"Hell, Barney, that's the Lord's day."

"Just don't be pocketing what ain't yours. Understand?"

"I got the bar. You take care of Miss Maddie."

Barney headed to the rear and stuck his head in the kitchen, where Gilda and Belle were working, and snapped at Belle, "Belle, you get upstairs and tend to Maddie."

"You want I should take her a cup of soup?"

"No, just follow me up."

Revenge of the Damned

He led the way and she obediently followed, but when he topped the stairs he blocked the way forward to Maddie's rooms, an adjoining pair next to where Belle's room had been, now occupied by Sadie.

"We ain't going that way," Barney said, and pointed to the far end of the hall where her small crib was.

"Maddie don't want you poking the girls. She tol' me—"

"What Maddie don't know won't hurt her, but you tell her and it'll hurt you…real bad. You owe me for hanging them what cut you."

Belle clamped her jaw, turned around, and walked to her room with Barney close behind.

***

Two men were seated at one of the half-dozen round tables and four more were belied up to the bar, but at a far end. Twodogs entered and the place quieted as all eyes fell on him. He carried his Winchester in one hand, and rested the other on the Remington Army he wore, and met every man's gaze one by one. Each of the miners, which they all seemed to be, cut their eyes away and went back to conversations they'd been carrying on when Twodogs had pushed through the batwings.

He moved to the bar, and eyed the toothless bartender, a weasel of a man, who wiped the bar on his way down.

"You drinkin'?" he asked.

Twodogs nodded. "Whiskey."

"You got money?"

"More than you got teeth," Twodogs said, and he wasn't smiling.

Henry, the bartender, clamped his mouth shut and grabbed a bottle of the cheap stuff and a glass, then filled the three-finger glass to the rim.

"Two bits," he said through tight lips.

Twodogs reached in a pocket and dug out a dollar and slammed it on the bar. "Leave bottle."

Henry nodded, did so, grabbed up the coin, and returned to the other end of the bar where the four miners were talking. But every so often one glanced at Twodogs, not quite sure of his intent.

But the big Indian seemed content to sip his whiskey.

***

As Belle had feared, Barney was not only huge and heavy, but mean. He shoved her legs in positions legs were not built to reach, then turned her to her stomach and with one ham sized hand on the back of her neck, shoved her down into the straw filled mattress until she could barely catch her breath—she was about to panic, afraid the wound on her face would be torn open.

He slipped off the bed to a standing position and dragged her up to her knees. At least she was able to catch a breath and the pain in her face and wound lessened.

Then he tried to violate her in a way she'd never allowed done. And she swung a hand back, trying to slap or claw him as she yelled, "No! No! Don't do that."

But rather than stop, he reached up and slapped her hard, then pushed her face down into the mattress again. She couldn't get a breath.

She kicked hard, catching him in a knee.

He grunted. But only shoved harder, meaning to have his way with her.

She screamed, and he hit her hard, a sledgehammer blow, on the back of the head. Fearing she would pass out, fearing for her life, she snaked a hand under her pillow and wrapped her hand around the butt of her little double-barrel belly gun.

She tried to scream a warning to him, to frighten him off. But he had her face buried and screaming with so much pain she was afraid she'd pass out from it, if not the lack of breath.

So she reached down to her side, and without seeing where she was aiming, fired up and back.

And he was off her. She spun to her back, gasping for air, and sat up. He was standing, staring in disbelief, one hand covering what was obviously a wound in his chest near his shoulder.

"You lousy bitch," he roared, and stepped forward, blood now seeping between the fingers of the hand covering the wound, but the other hand extended, fat corn cob sized fingers splayed out, going for her throat.

She aimed the gun again, cocking the second barrel in the same motion, and he hesitated. Then his face turned to scowl, and he lunged.

She aimed for his chest but as his knees hit the edge of the bed, her aim lifted and the .44 slug took him just under the left eye.

His hands flew up and backward as he slammed back against the wall, then eyes still open, blood spurting in heart driven dollops from under his eye, he slid down the wall and the bleeding stopped.

She slipped off the bed then went to the small chest she kept and dug into it—breaking and reloading the belly gun first thing—then digging out her warmest clothes. Canvas men's pants came on over wool long johns and a flannel shirt covered a chemise that bound her ample breasts. She threw a few more things in a small carpet bag, including the remaining gold she hadn't sewn into her heavy jacket. She heard footsteps outside her room, moving from room to room trying to locate where the shots originated. When she knew they were at the far front end of the hall, she peeked out to see Henry and two other men disappear into Maddie's room.

She put on her heavy coat, wrapped a wool scarf around her neck, then moved quickly out of her room, quietly closing the door, and down the back stairway. Henry, normally the swamper, was roomed in the last cubby hole near the back door.

She slipped into his room and helped herself to a pair of brogans that were too large for her, but only a size or two, and some woolen mittens that she stuffed into her coat's pockets.

Digging into her bag, she came up with a ten-dollar gold piece, and left it on Henry's cot. After peeking out his door, to make sure no one was in the back hall, she quickly opened the back door of Mattie's and ran outside into the darkness.

There was no question in her mind that these men, who'd paid good money to share her bed, would now be happy to share her eyes and hide with the crows and magpies as she swung from a rope, so she ran.

Chapter Forty

TWODOGS, AS DID ALL THE OTHER men in the saloon, heard the shots coming from the second story, but unlike all the others, who ran for the stairway, he finished his drink. With the quart bottle still half full, he re-corked it. Then he walked around the bar and found the small box tucked between two barrels of beer and relieved it of all the money it held.

He nodded with satisfaction, then walked back around, retrieved his half-full bottle of whiskey, and left. He tucked the whiskey into the pack saddle with his other goods, tightened the cinches, mounted, and headed up the mountain to where he'd left Dob in the thicket.

He was drunk, and realized it when he swayed in the saddle, then began singing a Crow song taught to him by his mother to ward off creatures who only venture out in darkness. Only three or four hundred yards up the mountain, he reined to a stop as something moved up ahead. He leaned forward, trying to make out what it was, only twenty or so paces ahead. Had he attracted one of those creatures with his terrible singing?

"Help!" Someone yelled at him and he jerked backwards and almost fell out of the saddle. "Help me, please," the voice came again, and he realized it was a woman. He spurred the animals forward until she stood only feet from him.

"Please help me. I can't go back to town."

"You shoot?" Twodogs asked, putting this woman and her trouble together with the shot back at the saloon. She didn't answer, so he asked again, "You shoot in saloon? Who you shoot?"

"A man was trying to hurt me badly," she said, and stepped even closer. At the same time she recognized him as an Indian, and he saw she was badly hurt.

"You're an Indian," she replied.

"Yes. Get on horse. I go warm cabin."

"On top that pack saddle?" she asked.

"You walk, if want. You stay, if want. I go now."

"No, please. I'll get up there somehow."

She moved to the side of the pack animal and got a foot and oversize brogan in between a cincha-pack-rope and the horse, and struggled atop and slightly to the rear of the load.

"Thank you," she said, when settled.

Twodogs gave heels to the pinto and started forward, taking up his singing again.

After a few hundred yards, he reined up, and frightened her as he yelled. "Dob...go now." He got no reply, then yelled even louder. "Dob!"

And to her surprise a man came limping out of the trees.

He struggled through the foot-deep snow, now slushy from the day's growing warmth, then stopped short. "By God you done give my seat to some owlhoot."

"Woman," Twodogs replied. "Woman hurt."

Dob struggled even closer. "You a woman?" he asked, trying to see in the darkness.

"Many a man knows me to be," she said. Then a chill ran down her back. There was something about this man that made her even more fearful than she was of the big Indian.

Had she jumped from frying pan into fire?

And Dob stumbled backward when he realized she was the bitch he'd cut. But she didn't seem to recognize who he was.

He turned to Twodogs. "How the hell we both gonna ride?"

"Not. Hang on to horse's tail. Then trade. She ride, you drag...you drag, she ride."

Revenge of the Damned

"It's too far," Dob said.

"You not know how far. Only an hour past where I found you. We go now."

"I ain't going."

"Good," Twodogs said. "I shoot you here. Rather have woman."

"No, no, I'll drag the first...say...three hundred steps, then we trade?"

Twodogs dismounted, leaving his Winchester in the boot. He dropped the lead rope away from the pack horse and tied a Spanish hackamore, then gave the woman the reins. "You lead out. I follow."

It was nearly dawn by the time they arrived at the Quinn place.

Both Belle and Dob were so exhausted and cold they made no argument when Twodogs led them into the barn rather than the cabin. The barn had a stove which Twodogs stoked up.

Belle was surprised when another man, covered in animal hides, raised up from a pallet across the room, "What did you bring us, Twodogs?"

"Woman. And Deputy Dob."

"Deputy?" Bama asked.

"Damn, ain't you..." Dob started to say he was the black in the poster, but then thought better of it.

"He harmless," Twodogs said, drawing a humph from Dob who was far too exhausted to complain any more.

Belle stood in front of the little pot belly, warming hands frozen even with the woolen gloves, looking as satisfied as if she were in the finest hotel in New Orleans. Dob stood beside her, making her very nervous because something about the man niggled at her. In fact, she got a chill down her back, and was happy with what the Indian did next.

When Dob turned to warm his front side, Twodogs unholstered his six shooter and closed the distance between them. A thump rang across the room as Twodogs cracked the back of the deputy's noggin. Dob went down in a heap.

"He's damn sure harmless now," Bama said, climbing slowly out from under the skins.

Twodogs crossed the barn to a rack holding tack and rope and came back and rolled Dob to his belly and hogtied him.

"Now harmless," Twodogs said, then added. "I sleep now."

"I'll be watching over Deputy Dob," Bama said, standing and stretching. Then he turned to Belle. "Ma'am, I'll not be need'n that there bed for a good long while, if you don't mind sleeping after an old mule skinner."

"That's very kind of you, sir," she said, "however you look more like a handsome thespian than a man of the trail," and quickly crossed the room and snuggled into the skins.

Bama moved near Twodogs who was settling into his own pile of skins. "You bring the cartridges and the vittles?"

"I did."

"And you brought a woman."

"I did. She would die in snow. She have trouble in Junket City."

"I could see that by her face. That's a hell of a wound."

"Think maybe she got even."

"You want me to wake you when Abby cooks?" Bama asked.

"Noon. Sleep now."

"I do believe you done earned it," Bama said. Then he asked, "What the devil is a thespian?"

Twodogs shrugged and climbed into his bed, pulling skins up to his chin..

Bama shook his head, wondering if he'd been complimented or insulted, then went to unpack and grain the exhausted animals.

Chapter Forty One

JOAQUIN GUZMAN, Stanley McCallester, with Simon and Hugh Tollofson set out an hour after sunup, after filling their bellies with steak, eggs, potatoes and coffee at the Cattlemen's. The weather was continuing to warm, with the snow gone from Helena and only beginning a couple of hundred feet higher in elevation. They each rode geldings near sixteen hands tall and each led an animal. Two pack horses and the two Percherons followed.

McCallester, a renowned sniper in the recent hostilities, carried a .45/.90 Sharps with double set triggers and a ladder rear sight. With a thirty inch barrel it was hard to carry in a saddle boot so it was stowed on a pack-horse, wrapped tightly in a small carpet. McCallester was credited with a dozen kills over six hundred yards, and two nearing a thousand, with the Enfield he carried during the war. It was said he'd kill anything that moved in his field of fire, then laugh and cackle for a half hour after making a shot—man, woman, horse, dog— it didn't matter to McCallester, he just liked killing.

And he was very good at it.

Wentworth stood on his porch and watched them go, and was glad of it.

They'd only been in town one night, and it was one night too many. He'd had to Take old Billy Scroggins to jail, even though he knew it was the Tollofsons who were at fault. Billy was the swamper at Sadie's Saloon, which was far more a pleasure house than a drinking establishment. Billy had failed to empty a spittoon and Hugh Tollofson had a boot soaked with tobacco juice when his brother had knocked it over. Rather than take it out on his brother, Hugh Tollofson had slapped poor old Billy around, shaming him something awful. Rather than cause trouble with his new hired hands, Wentworth took Billy to spend the night in jail…after Tollofson told him Billy had pulled a knife. Wentworth knew Willy didn't carry gun or knife—probably didn't own one—but it was better to keep the peace. Besides, Billy probably ate better in jail than in the shack he lived in behind Sadie's.

***

I awake before the sun is up and move quietly out of Abby's room to make coffee. As usual, as soon as I'm stirring around, Jed appears at the head of the steep stairs and nearly flies down.

"What's up today, Linc?" the boy asks.

"The only thing left to complete on the wagon is the tongue and some hardware. Bama is working on the harness…traces and reins and has salvaged enough from your pa's scrap pile to make a fine wagon. We've shined up some collars and a double tree. We'll be hooking up a couple of horses this afternoon, God willing and this weather holds. "

I've seen the boy up the hillside at his father's grave, now buried in three feet of snow, and am wondering how the boy will take leaving the only home he's ever known, so I ask him, "Jed, it's a long way to Oregon or Washington. You up for such a trip?"

"My pa said he wanted to see Oregon…I guess I'll do it for him. We can't go far unless this weather warms up, can we?"

"We should get at least one thaw before winter really sets in. This early cold is unusual. If the weather breaks, we'll head west and make Missoula at least."

"The coffee is boiling. We got any sugar left?"

Revenge of the Damned

"The vittles we sent Twodogs after were on the table when I poked my head out. There's no cream as the cow's quit on us. Can you handle just sugar?"

"Time I growed up, I guess—"

"Grew up," Abby says from her bedroom.

"Okay, ma, done grew up," Jed says with a laugh.

"It's time I grew up, not done grew up, young man."

"Yes'um," he says, and looks at me and both of us laugh.

I grab the pot and a couple of mugs and head out to the barn, and quickly discover I haven't grabbed enough mugs.

A man, tied to a roof support post, is awake, and is begging Bama to untie him. Twodogs, asleep, is snoring loudly. And a woman, obvious by the long wine red tresses flowing over the skins where she lays, where Bama normally beds down, is sleeping quietly with her face turned to the barn wall.

"You fellas had a busy night," I say, somewhat astonished.

"You're Dolan?" the man asks, then getting a nod, continues, "These som'bitches got me tied up here for nothing. I was a peaceful traveler and was waylaid by that redskin over younder—"

"Hold on. I'll get your story when Twodogs comes around. You can have a cup of this coffee, but your feet are staying tied up." I turn to Bama, "You know what's going on here?"

Bama shruggs, then says, "This here's a Wentworth man...a deputy. Dob he says he's called. That lady over there is from Junket City, where she be runnin' from some trouble." Then he notes the cups and pot. "Coffee. I'd be obliged..."

I pour the two mugs and hand one to Bama, free Dob's hands and offer him the other.

"What did you do to my Indian friend, deputy?" I ask Dob.

"Not a damn thing. And I ain't no deputy no more. I done quit and was riding for Deer Lodge or Missoula when my horses run off and this redskin come along and friended me, or so I thought. You can let me untie my feet now and with the loan of a horse I'll be on my way—"

"Not untying you, sure as hell not loaning you an animal as we only got one apiece. I'll bring you out some vittles in a while. You just set quiet while Mister Twodogs gets his rest."

Dob was quiet for a minute, then snaps at me. "You better be right good to me, Dolan. Wentworth and a whole gob of mean-as-hell deputies are likely heading up the mountain right now, and they got a new judge in town who's known to hang fellas without waiting for another sun up."

"New judge?"

"Yep, some fella from back east…Peabody. Horace, I think his given name."

"General Horace Peabody?"

"I heard something about his being a Union general before he come west."

I turn to Bama. "I'll bring you out some chow as soon as Abby gets it on the table. Maybe you ought to stay with the deputy and retie his hands when he finishes his coffee."

"I ain't no deputy no more."

"Stay with this fella until I can relieve you or until Twodogs comes around. How about the woman?"

"You know as much as I do," Bama said with another shrug of his big shoulders.

I head for the house with lots more to think about. Judge Horace Peabody…General Horace Peabody.

That could be the answer to my problems.

Possibly heaven sent.

Chapter Forty Two

JOAQUIN GUZMAN AND HIS CREW plodded up the mountain until the snow got two feet deep, then found a thick stand of fir and Guzman and McCallester left the Tollofson brothers and the guide Wentworth had provided with a warm fire and their mounts, saddled the two big Percherons, transferred McCallester's Sharps to his mount, and continued where the guide suggested. They'd come across the tracks of two animals plowing through the snow with someone following on foot, and decided it was as good a trail as any to follow as it went up the mountain where the guide said there was a cabin...the Quinn cabin.

***

Wentworth had given them careful directions to the two cabins on this, the north side of the mountain. With the weather as it had been, he figured Dolan must have holed up in a cave or, more likely, he'd come across one of the two cabins. The old Williamson place was empty, but was still decent shelter with a good stone fireplace and even a stack of firewood, and the Quinn place had all a fellow on the run could ask for. Wentworth cared little for Twodogs, even though he was sure it was the Indian who'd murdered the barber. Bama, the black, was a much more deserving catch as he'd murdered a federal judge, and the Marshal would be expected to pursue him with vigor. But his interest in Dolan was personal.

The hired manhunters had barely ridden out of town when Tiny Allendorf from the Cattlemen's, Howard Polkinghorn one of Helena's new millionaire miners, Delbert O'Brien likewise, and the mayor, Johnathan P. Dougle showed up in his office. They represented a majority of the town council. Wentworth was a little surprised to see Judge Stanley's son, attorney Norval Stanley, in tow with the town's finest.

"What's up?" Wentworth asked.

"Norval here tells us his ma, Evelyn, has recanted her belief that the big black fellow was the one killed the judge, Crazy Willy, and Deputy Phinias."

"I thought that was settled? She saw the black with the guns in hand and the three of them laying kilt."

"That was sure enough what she testified," the mayor said, with a shrug, "but she's been waking up at night after dreaming the same dream, and that's seeing the black fella with nothing but an ax in hand and the Judge and Crazy Willy shooting it out like they were at Gettysburg. She was at the kitchen window when it happened."

Wentworth was a little dumbstruck, then he laughed. "We're to believe some grief-stricken woman's dreams? Hell, we got posters out on the boy."

"Hell no," the mayor said, "should Guzman and his killers shoot him down we'll owe them the reward for killing an innocent man."

Finally, Norval Stanley spoke up. "My mother may be grief stricken, but she's the most level headed soul you'll ever meet, and, if she's come too the conclusion he's innocent, then he's innocent. You don't want a man's blood on your hands."

Wentworth guffawed. "Hell, he's a nigra. Likely worthless as tits on a boar. It'll damn sure be an accident he gets filled fulla holes."

To Norval's credit, he stepped up almost chest to chest with the bigger man. "He's a man, and you'd better get those posters down and send somebody after that bunch of killers and call them off this innocent man or I'll go on a rampage with our new judge and the governor and whoever else might listen."

Wentworth merely glared at him for a moment, then finally replied in a low voice, "We'll get them flyers down in due time. You want to ride after them boys and call them off, you got my permission. Now, get out of my face a'fore I forget you just lost your daddy."

But Norval didn't back down. He had his hackles up and snapped, "By all that's holy, I will ride after them. I'll get some help and go this very afternoon."

"Don't freeze your ass off, Norval," Wentworth snickered, turning away and heading for his desk.

***

I return from the barn with my mind swirling. General Horace Peabody could be the answer to my prayers, I decide as I enter the cabin to consult with Abby. She's talked me into moving on west if the snow clears before real winter settles on the land, and I've agreed, but this may change things drastically. I take a seat and speak as she stands at the stove, flipping flapjacks.

"You're gonna need a few more," I say.

"You extra hungry or what?" she asks, giving me a smile and a wink.

"Twodogs brought a couple more visitors."

"What?" That stops her and she turns with hands on hips. "We don't have supplies to last the winter with two more."

"One of them is tied to a post, a deputy from town. The other is a woman. A lady of color who, as I understand it, was a soiled dove from down Junket City way. It seems Twodogs sort of rescued her as she was on the run. Her face is cut up and she had some trouble down at Matties."

Abby sighs deeply. "I swear, this place is getting to be a home for the wayward."

"There's more."

Another deep sigh. "I hope that wasn't the good news and now the bad?"

"Nope. Could be very good news. Let me show you something..." I disappear into Abby's room and dig into my pack, then return and walk over and hand her a circular medallion with a star embossed on it. It is strung on a blue ribbon.

"Pretty," she says, "What is it?"

"Finish cooking your flapjacks and I'll take a load of 'em out to the barn. Twodogs and the woman, and likely the deputy, are sleeping so it'll only be Bama. I'll come back and while we're eating give you the whole story."

"I'll bet it's a good one," Abby says, shaking her head and I'll bet she's wondering just what it is I haven't told her.

Chapter Forty Three

"SO, WHAT IS THIS PRETTY little trinket with the blue ribbon?" Abby asks when we're seated in front of a platter of flapjacks. Jed has joined us.

"Well, ma'am, it's a medal I was given for doing what lots of other fellows were doing, but for some reason they singled me out."

"Medal for what?" she asks, her interest rising. Jed stops chewing and looks up from his plate.

"As I recall, and I quote, recognition to men who distinguished themselves conspicuously by gallantry and intrepidity in combat with an enemy of the United States. That's a lot of fancy talk for what damn near every man on the battlefield, on both sides, was doing every damn day of the war."

She is quiet for a moment, then asks, "Exactly what did you do?" Jed doesn't say a word, merely listens without a twitch.

"I don't much like to talk about the war, but you asked. So here goes. I was with Sherman and we had the rebs by the throat. Even though old reb General Joseph E. Johnston had managed to scrape up over twenty thousand men it was a fool's errand to confront Sherman's forces as we marched through North Carolina.

"General Johnston's plan was to overwhelm us...us being a column separated from Sherman. I was with General Henry

W. Slocum's two-corps column, and we were separated by ten miles from the rest of Sherman's forces.

"On the morning, and I recall it as if it was yesterday...the morning of March 19, 1865, our column clashed with Confederate cavalry just south of Bentonville. We pushed back the Southern horsemen until we found ourselves under attack by rebel infantry. Slocum quickly consolidated our troops, and I'd captured a reb myself who'd been riding a fine tall black horse with white socks. While our boys beat off Johnston's all day attacks with hard fighting, General Slocum sent me on that reb's horse to beg Sherman for help. I rode all night, having that fine horse shot out from under me and then capturing another horse, having to kill a reb colonel in the doing of it, and getting myself a little shot up. After dark, Johnston pulled his men back to a good defensive position. But I'd gotten to Sherman and rode with General Oliver Howard back to aid our boys.

"Eventually, wanting to rejoin my own, I busted on ahead, and back through the reb lines to advise Slocum that Howard and his boys would be hitting Johnston on the left flank. Then, I guess, with loss of blood, I passed out. I awoke in a hospital well behind the lines and a couple of weeks later I'd healed enough to stand. General Peabody himself was there tying that blue ribbon around my neck and saying I was a hero. Hell, any of our boys would have done the same."

"I doubt that," she said.

"We outnumbered those reb boys by three or four to one, but they were tough. The next day Sherman's men attacked the Rebel left flank. They were repulsed and we were nose to nose all night, when Johnston pulled back toward Smithfield. I was out of the war with a hole in my side, a hole in my shoulder, and this little medal. As far as I'm concerned, this honor was for all of us...mostly for those still out there, buried.

"Usually it's the president hangs one of these on a fella, but I guess he was tied up with the war. Peabody was his adjutant and came all the way from Washington to do me and some other bluecoats the honor."

"I'm just glad you lived through it," Abby said. Getting up from her plate she circled the table and hugged and kissed me.

When she returned to her seat, I continued. "So, I've got to go to Helena."

She suddenly glared at me. "I thought you'd given up revenging your former fiancé?"

"It's not that, Abby, although to be truthful it niggles at me every day. General Peabody, the man who presented me with this here medal of honor is now the federal judge in Helena. He's the one man on earth who'd likely believe what I've got to say about Wentworth…about what happened in Helena."

"You ride in there, they'll hang you."

"I won't just ride in. I'll slip in and find General Peabody…Judge Peabody, where I can talk without shooting up half the town."

"We can just head out when the snow clears—"

"And forever be looking over our shoulders to see if some bounty hunter or lawman has a shotgun leveled on us. I got to try and make this right, Abby. For you, Jed, and myself."

She was quiet for a long moment, then nodded. "You're likely right."

"I'll go first thing in the morning."

***

Guzman and McCallester had been trading off the lead, though following the tracks left by Twodogs, Dob, and Pearl wasn't difficult. They reached a plateau, with the mountain still rising high above them, when Guzman reined up.

"Smoke," he said, pointing up a ravine than dumped a stream onto the flat. The snow on the north side of the mountain was still a foot and a half deep, but seemed a fairly easy task for the big Percherons.

"Stay alert," Guzman said, and gigged his big horse forward. After moving up a gentle slope alongside a small stream for a couple of hundred yards, a meadow opened in front of them. "Smoke is coming from the north side of the meadow, maybe another two hundred yards," Guzman said, waving McCallester forward. "Time to ride quiet," Guzman said. "You move up the slope on the south side...somewhere you get a view of the cabin. This should be the Quinn place. We got three or four hours till dark. You get a bead on things with that Sharps and I'll go up the other side and wait a bit. Maybe a half hour or forty five minutes I'll wander down and see what I can see, then bang on the door like I was just passing through."

"Should I pull off on one of them poster boys, should I see him?"

"Damn straight. Dolan and the black are wanted dead or alive on the posters. Dead's a damn sight less trouble."

McCallester merely nodded, then reined left and moved across the small stream and disappeared into the willows.

Guzman rolled one and lit up, sitting quietly for most of thirty minutes, until he was sure McCallester was set up on the slope above where the smoke originated, then flipped his butt into the stream and gave gentle heels to the big Percheron. The meadow widened and soon he spotted the small corral, with a milk cow and five horses. He rode casually, as it he hadn't a worry in the world, until he could see the barn. Then he saw the cabin, set a little closer to the north side where the mountain rose only a hundred feet or so behind. Across the meadow, where the cabin faced, the mountain rose at least another two thousand feet.

Guzman reined the Percheron up thirty paces from the front door. As he cut his eyes around—the sign of a hunter, and a cautious one—smoke rose from a stack at both the cabin and the barn.

As he knew no one here would recognize him, unless they'd ridden up from Helena the last two days, he called out.

"Hello the cabin!" He got no immediate response so he yelled even louder. "Howdy in the house. You got coffee for a cold traveler?"

Chapter Forty Four

JED AND I ARE PERCHED AT the table playing checkers when the voice rings out. Abby puts aside some mending and rises from a rocking chair at the same time Jed does.

"No, Jed. You get up to the loft," then she turns to me as I'm disappearing into her room. I return with my Golden Boy in hand and a revolver strapped to my waist by the time she reaches the door and has it ajar.

"And who might you be?" she calls out the door, then turns to me. I've taken up a position at the window without glass in the panes. "You know him?" she asks, and I answer with a shake of my head. "He looks to be alone," she says.

I shove the shutters open just enough to see, or get a barrel out. "Looks don't count much. There's lots of places to hide out there."

"Just traveling through," the man on the big horse calls out, then repeats, "You got a little coffee to spare a tired and cold traveler. I done come from over the mountain, over Deer Lodge way."

I catch some movement on the barn side of the window and turn just in time to see Twodogs, a revolver in hand stepping forward. Then almost as quickly, he slams backward, the revolver flung aside and the report of a big rifle rocks the shutters.

My stomach does a flip flop and heat floods my backbone. I've seen a lot of men take a bullet and know this one hit the big Indian dead center.

"Get away from the door," I yell at Abby, then turn my attention back to the man on the horse, but he's already given heels to the animal and is throwing snow up behind him as he disappears.

"A posse you think?" Abby calls to me as I'm visually searching the hillside across the creek.

"Don't know," I answer, without taking my eyes off the slope.

"Where'd that shot go?" she calls to me from her new location in the doorway to her room.

"Twodogs came out of the barn with gun in hand. It wasn't the rider shot him. There's at least one more across the creek somewhere. You get down lower Abby, in case they try a couple through the door."

"How about me," Jed says, from up the steep stairway. I can see the boy has armed himself with his little rolling block.

"You stay up in the loft, Jed and stay low, understand."

"Yes, sir," the boy replies, and kneels on the upper floor.

Then the first rider's voice rings out from somewhere to the side, a place away from the barn, a place we can't see from door or windows. "My name is Guzman…Joaquin Guzman. I'm a deputy of the law from Helena, duly deputized by the Marshal. I see you're harboring a wanted man, who I believe is now shot dead. If y'all don't want to join him, I'd suggest you toss out whatever arms you might have and come on out with your hands empty and in the air."

"Let me talk to him," Abby says, moving forward to the door.

"I'd rather you have your say out of the line of fire," I snap, but she ignores me and cracks the door open again.

She calls out, "Mister…Mister Gooseman, is that right?"

"It's Guzman. I presume you're Mrs. Quinn?"

"I am, and you have shot down a man who was helping about the place. I'd like to tend to him?"

"No need. He's been holed dead center in the breast bone by a Sharps forty five ninety. You could ride my Percheron through the hole in that man."

"Then take him and go, if that's what you want?"

"He weren't nothing. A lousy twenty five dollars. I want a fella name of Lincoln Dolan and another, a black goes by the handle Bama. You send them out and we'll be on our way, la ti da."

"You are mighty cavalier about having just murdered a man."

"Ma'am, I don't know nothing about cavalier, but I do know I'm not leaving without these other two fellas."

"I've never heard of either of them, Mister Guzman."

"You got a fire in the cabin and a fire in the barn. That speaks to me of more fellas about."

"Mister Twodogs, my hand, the man you've killed, lived in the barn. There's no one there now."

"I'm not accustomed to calling a lady a liar, Mrs. Quinn, but that barn door was pulled shut by someone after that dirty Indian was shot dead. I guess you want me to believe it was his spirt flying back inside."

"No reason for sarcasm, Mister Guzman. There's a bit of a breeze out there and I'm sure the door merely blew shut."

He is quiet for a moment, then his voice becomes more gruff. "Look, lady, you come on out here with your hands in the air, and bring your whelp with you."

"Mister Guzman, I'm a woman alone without a man on the place, now that you've murdered my helper. You wouldn't want your wife or mother—"

"Don't have no wife and my mama done met her maker. So, you just come on out and I won't have to burn that place down around your ears."

"Step out where I can see you, Mister Guzman. How do I know you're not a road agent. I presume you have some kind of badge if you're truly a deputy?" Abby turns to me, and speaks in a low voice. "Are you watching for him?"

I'm at the window, but back far enough that the barrel of my Golden Boy is unseen. I nod in answer to her question.

Guzman yells again, "You're beginning to try my patience, Mrs. Quinn. Step on outside or I'll light your cabin afire."

I can see the Percheron, tied to a lodgepole pine next to the meadow, and presume the man, Guzman, is nearby but have yet to spot him.

"Please don't do that, Mister Guzman. My young son is here and no one else."

"Bullshit," Guzman yells, and then I make out some movement in the nearby copse of trees, mostly lodgepole, but some thick elderberry line the meadow, making it almost impossible to make out anything beyond. The branches of the berry bushes are still lined with brown leaves, those you can see that aren't snow covered.

Then I catch a flash of brown canvas and realize Guzman is moving around, trying to gather up enough dry brush to start a fire. Then, in moments, I see flame flare up. Before I can count ten, a short stocky man with swarthy complexion pushes thru the bushes, rifle in one hand and a flaming bough in the other and runs for Abby's woodpile, against the east wall of the cabin. Two boxes of tinder rest there, and I surmise them to be the man's target.

But the thick chested man only gets ten steps into the clearing when the Golden Boy bucks in my hands and the man spins, going down on top his own hastily contrived torch. He rolls to the side, then the shutter near my face splinters and I drop to the ground as if I'd been poleaxed with an ax handle.

Abby screams and runs to me, but I scramble her way and, rising, pull her up against the thick log wall.

And I'm unhurt.

"Somebody's up the hill across the way with a big rifle...likely a Sharps. Guzman is down, although I think I hit him a little low. I've got to check."

I crab back across the floor, keeping well below the level of the window sill, then stand, but behind the logs and not in front of the shutters, and reach out and push the one nearest open. Almost as soon as it flies back, another heavy bullet wings through the opening and slams into Abby's Buck stove, cracking the oven door.

"If you don't kill him, I will," Abby snaps with such determination I fear she'll run out the door with her broom and go after the man with the Sharps.

Chapter Forty Five

"GUZMAN'S DOWN, but crawling away," I say. "He left his rifle where he fell. Now, let's hope there's only one more up the hill."

Almost as soon as I say it I hear a blood chilling scream coming from the edge of the woods up the hillside. I can't help myself and look, but rather than rise to the same window I run in front of the door and cross to the window with glass panes. Its outside shutters are open and it is only covered with heavy curtains made by Abby of multiple layers of flour sack cloth.

"That sounded like the devil his'sef latched onto that old boy." I'm not too far from wrong, as watching I can see something coming down the hill, then realize it's Bama, and he has a man by the ankle and is dragging him, bouncing and yelling, over downfall and through snow piles. When he reaches the bottom he doesn't stop, but rather drags the man through the creek and right up to the cabin door.

Bama drops the man's leg and I step into the doorway and wave Bama inside. "The other one could still have a weapon," I caution, then realize the man on the ground has an arm that's bent in a way an arm shouldn't bend.

"That fella have an accident?" I ask with a smile.

"Yep," Bama says, "he done run into me while he was looking to shoot you. I twisted his arm a mite. You want I should go after the other one?"

"I'll go, you get back to watching that deputy in the barn. Check on Twodogs on the way, but...I pray to God I'm wrong...I'm fairly sure there's no helping him."

We go out the door at almost the same time, Bama turning left toward the barn, me right toward the copse of trees. It won't be hard to find the fella who calls himself Guzman, as he was dragging himself through snow and mud until the snow deepened up against the trees...but I don't follow. It isn't wise to track a wounded animal in his own trail as he's likely to be watching and laying for you.

Instead I break to the right and move up the slope behind the cabin, then east where I can see down into the trees from slightly above.

In moments I see a man's legs sticking out from under the low boughs of a pine, and move as quietly as possible down toward them. When a couple of dozen paces from the still protruding legs, I shout out.

"If you're not dead, Guzman, you soon will be. I believe you still have a sidearm, and if you want help with that hole in your hide, throw it out and the woman can tend to you."

"Eat dung, you son of a bitch. You shot me."

"I shot some son of a bitch who was carrying a torch to burn down a lady's cabin with her and her son inside. Sounds to me, and most would agree, that's a fella need'n shooting."

"Damn if I don't believe I need some doctor help," Guzman says, following it with a low groan. "I'm throwing out. Don't you shoot me."

"Hell, Guzman, them fat legs of yours been stickin' out. If I wanted to hole you some more you wouldn't ever be trotting to the outhouse again."

A fine nickel plated Sheriff's Model Colt flies out into the snow. As I move forward, carefully, as a man who Guzman appears to be would likely carry a belly gun as well.

Just as I get where he could see under the boughs, another voice rings out, "Drop that rifle, please."

Revenge of the Damned

I freeze. It's an educated voice, not one you'd expect coming from a trapper or woodsman. Could Guzman have more help?

"Who the hell are you?" I call over my shoulder, and lower the muzzle of my rifle as I start to turn.

"Don't," the man yells. "Don't turn around until you drop the rifle. There are three guns on you."

I comply and turn to see a man in a fancy sheepskin coat, and two others, both in rougher attire.

"I'm Norval Stanley, Judge Stanley's son. I'm here to call Guzman and his men off that Bama fella. My mother has stood up for the black, saying he had nothing to do with the death of my father, Crazy Willy, or the deputy. Now, who are you?"

Before I can answer, another voice rings out from above and behind me. "You fellas drop them rifles so I don't haf'ta actually kill someone."

The three of them don't move, but their eyes search the trees. Then another voice rings out. "Do like he says. I'm a woman, but I can shoot this scatter gun and it'll likely cut y'all in half." Then another voice, a third one, another female, "And I'm not bad with this Winchester—" and she is interrupted by a boy, "And I can shoot the eye out of a tree squirrel at fifty yards."

The three men carefully place their weapons in the snow.

"And the gun belts," I advise. "Those ladies get a little nervous with their trigger fingers."

The men quickly comply.

"You gonna get me patched up?" Guzman's voice rings out from under the branches.

"You three fellas can earn your keep by carrying Mister Guzman into the cabin."

As Norval Stanley and his fellow riders dig under the pine to pull Guzman out, Bama, Abby, Belle, and Jed move out of the trees into sight.

"Y'all are a pretty sight," I say, eyeing each of them in turn.

They give young Mister Stanley a hard look.

"You're here for what reason exactly?" I inquire. He's holding Guzman by one arm, and ignores my question.

"We best get this man where we can cauterize his wound. He's bleeding like a stuck hog," says Stanley.

"You didn't walk here," I say.

"Horses are back in the trees a hundred yards or so. We heard the shooting and hoofed it here."

I turn to Jed and Bama, "If you gentlemen will gather up their firearms and horses I'll escort them to the cabin."

The two with Stanley are shaking in their boots, as if I'm going to shoot them in their tracks, so as they walk ahead of the ladies and me, I reassure them, "You fellas mind your manners and we'll have no trouble. I want to hear more about just why you've come calling."

They look even more frightened when we reach the cabin and see the man Bama dragged down the mountain, bound and tied with his back against the corral rail, his arm still canted like it was stomped on by a buffalo bull.

And he's moaning like a bull in a corral full of bright eyed young heifers.

"Looks like you ladies have some nursing to do," I say but the lady I presume is Belle, objects.

"I've never treated a broken bone," she says.

"I have, many an arm and leg, and helped in the removal of a few," Abby says. She turns to the young men accompanying Stanley. "You two get this man in the cabin and set him in the far corner over on the floor." She throws them a large kitchen towel. "Bind him tightly until I get a hot iron." Then she points to the man tied to the corral fencepost. "Then get that man inside and lay him on my table." Then snaps at Stanley, "You fetch a bucket of water while I get my stove to burning bright, if that hooligan didn't ruin it. I ought to jerk his arm off and beat him with it."

I can't help but smile, and promise myself to remember not to mess with Miss Abby's kitchen appliances.

But we've lost Twodogs; although strange in his ways he never did us anything but right. In fact he saved my bacon by not giving me up to the posse. So, no matter what other wrongs he might have done, I hope he's in his heaven an hour before the devil knows he's dead.

I'll pray over him.

Chapter Forty Six

ABBY BUILDS THE FIRE UP and shoves a poker in it to heat. We place Guzman on his butt in a corner with a cloth wrapped tightly around his middle to try and quell the bleeding, but he is getting mighty white in the face and I worry he'll bleed out. I don't want that to happen, as he wears a small copper badge and is likely the deputy he claims to be. I stand in the opposite corner and watch over all with my Golden Boy in hand.

Now that we're inside and Stanley has delivered the water, and the man with the arm is on his back on the table, I turn to the young men. "You'll find a pick and shovel in the barn, and a man tied there. Leave him tied. He'll be going out of here with you three and these two, should you all mind your manners. There's a dead man outside, a friend of ours, and you're going to wrap him in a couple of saddle blankets and bury him…with the same respect you'd pay your own pa…out in the meadow."

"Yes, sir," one of the young men says, and they shuffle to the door.

I call after them. "Don't mess with the man tied in the barn. You likely know him. I don't want to have to dig a hole for y'all."

They nod and hurry out.

Abby instructs Stanley and Belle. "You get the coat and shirt off Mister Guzman and get him on his face on the floor."

They do as instructed and Abby applies a red hot poker to the bleeding exit wound in his lower back. Mister Guzman, I decide, could shame a screech owl, and does so, twice, as they roll him to his back and do the same to the smaller entry wound. The smell is obviously something Norval Stanley can barely abide, not that anyone would appreciate the scorching sizzle and stench of cooked man-flesh.

It's obvious Guzman will be no trouble for a while as he's passed out cold.

Abby then directs their attention to the man with the twisted arm. Abby tries to soothe him as she might a rattlesnake. "I wish I had a quart of whiskey for you, but to be truthful you killed my friend, Mister Twodogs, and I don't much give a damn if this pains you." She glances up at Belle. "You're going to put all your weight on his off shoulder to hold him down." As she says it, the door opens and Bama fills it with his wide shoulders. She waves him over. "Hold his legs." Then she turns to Stanley. "Put a foot in his armpit and give this arm a steady pull. I'll align the bone then tell you to ease it back. Don't pay a lick of attention to his yelling."

Stanley does so and she works the man's upper arm bone into alignment, while the man does just as she expected. He screams so loud dust motes drift down from the ceiling.

Young Mister Stanley moves over to Abby's rocking chair and flops down, looking as if he would soon lose his lunch. I figure this is a good time to get the truth out of him, so I start grilling him.

"Now, Stanley, tell me the truth. Why are you here?"

"Wentworth acted as if he could care less if that Bama fella got hung or shot dead for killing my father. But my mother totally recanted her testimony and said he had nothing to do with my pa's death…and I came to intercept Guzman and his men…by the way, there are two more of his posse on down the mountain at some sort of base camp. Anyway, I'm glad to see this Bama in one piece."

"So, your mission is Good Samaritan?"

"Only that."

"And the two young fellas with you?"

"Paid to guide me and track Guzman."

"I'm taking you at your word. Some townsman of yours is out in the barn tied up. Dob, I think his name is—"

"Dob! Damn if he's not a fugitive like Mister Bama was. He rode off after making some charges he wasn't authorized to make and is a horse thief as well."

"What a bowl of worms we got up here on this mountain. Are you a man of your word, Mister Stanley?"

"I am, sir."

"I'm going to leave you out in the barn with all these fellas. Miss Abby and Miss Belle will cook for y'all but you'll be in the barn and stay in the barn. I'm leaving here in the morning…you don't happen to know where Judge Peabody is staying?"

"He was at the Cattlemen's, but he was moving to Mrs. Alice Crutchfield's boarding house."

"Fine. I'm riding out of here in the morning. You'll give me your word you won't start down the mountain until day after tomorrow, so I can get my business done with Judge Peabody—"

"You mean him no harm?" he asks, alarmed that he's told me the judge's likely location.

"The man may be my salvation, so the last thing I mean is to harm him."

He nods. "You keep us fed and housed and you have my word."

"Good."

Abby speaks up. "I wish I thought it good," she says, shaking her head.

All but Guzman and his man eat a big helping of elk stew and biscuits and we leave them to do for themselves and Dob in the warm, well heated barn.

In the morning I mean to ride down the mountain and find a way to have a quiet conversation with the man who stood in for the president and hung a medal of honor around my neck.

Let's hope that stands for something.

Chapter Forty Seven

THE YOUNG MEN DO A good job planting Twodogs, snow cleared away, a nice even mound, and even a cross at the head of his grave. I wish I knew more about the Crow way of sending their dead to the next life, but don't so we do the best we can. Just after sun up Pearl, Bama, Abby, Jed and I gather at his spot in the meadow—next to Abby's and Jed's, fairly recently, departed Mister Quinn. He's no longer alone in his meadow resting place. Abby reads the 23rd Psalm from the Good Book.

I spend a moment with Bama, telling him he's responsible to make sure there's no trouble from Guzman, his man who we've found out is McCallester, Stanley, and his two guides.

He gives me a grin, flashing white teeth, and informs me, "They's a fine Sharps rifle up the mountain I am to fetch. And those two Percherons will pull a wagon better'n any oxen or mules."

Then I spend a moment with Jed, telling him I'm counting on him to take care of his mother, but there's no need for the talk. He's proven to be more man than most men twice his age. And now she now has Belle to keep her company and hopefully be of help. I've noticed that Bama has taken a real shine to the lady, and it seems, she to him.

I spend more time with Abby, who again questions my decision to return to Helena and the possibility of getting right with the law. I'd doubt the possibility so long as the law is such as it is in Helena…but the fact is, Judge Peabody carries more weight than Marshal Wentworthless, or even the governor, in many ways.

Then, with two day's provisions, I head for my horse and a trek to see if I can make peace with the law…and think I likely can, should Marshal Oscar Wentworth stay out of the equation, which, unfortunately, is not likely.

The weather is mild as I let my dun pick his way down the mountain, careful to ride clear of Mullan Road until I'm well west of where Guzman confessed, on threat of me taking the hot iron to him again, his other two men were encamped. I do spot smoke and figure it's their fire. I'm able to join the road a few miles west of Helena, a road I'm happy to say is free of snow. Then, seeing a wagon coming my way, I'm forced to retreat into the fir forest again. But it's widely spaced and with the snow no longer a factor, easy traveling.

I fear riding into town in the daylight, and stay shy of any buildings until the sun is well below the mountains to the west. Even though the judge has moved on to Crutchfield's Boarding House, I'll be surprised if he's not in the town's classiest drinking establishment, The Cattlemen's. I tie my horse in back of Beauregard's Bucket of Blood, a block away from the Gulch and the Cattlemen's. I've worn a heavy scarf and borrowed a wide brimmed hat, formerly Mister Quinn's, and keep my coat collar turned up and the scarf wrapped so my face barely shows. I'm carrying my Golden Boy and wearing a Remington Army revolver, but it's not unusual to see a man carrying a rifle and walking about town as you don't want to leave an expensive piece in a saddle scabbard and have some lay-about relieve you of it.

It's still chilly enough that I don't look out of place in heavy coat and scarf.

I silently chide Tiny Allendorf, who's listed as proprietor on a sign near the saloon's batwing doors, as the windows need a good washing and it's difficult to make out the patrons through them, particularly through a cloud of cigar smoke. The restaurant and hotel have separate entrances and sets of windows—and the hotel seems more nicely shined. But, to my dismay, Judge Peabody is not taking his super at the establishment. So, I amble on down the boardwalk and kill some time investigating another half dozen establishments until I find myself in front of the Masonic Lodge. As memory serves me, the judge has set up temporary quarters in the lodge and, as the courthouse is under construction, the lodge is rented, as needed, to serve as courtroom.

Could he be working late and still at his desk? I stroll up the steps as if I belong there and cup my hands beside my eyes and press up against a pane to see into the well-lit lodge, and find myself almost face to face with the wide nose of Marshal Oscar Wentworth.

Luckily my hot breath has fogged the glass and I spin away, moving to the rail and lean over. The door opens and, obviously, he's not recognized me as he stomps past and down the stairs. He glances back but I've covered my face and am coughing as if I have reason to do so.

My palm is itching badly, wanting to be scratched with the butt of my Colt, but I quell the urge. Even more important than shooting the arrogant son of a bitch is palavering with Territorial Judge Horace J. Peabody, and picking a fight right here in Last Chance Gulch may get me a hearing with Peabody, but not the kind I'd like.

So, I bide my time and let Wentworth get a half block ahead, then follow until he turns into the restaurant door of the Cattlemen's. I glance up, and to my pleasant surprise the judge is coming my way and hard to miss in his modestly high stovepipe hat—reminiscent of President Lincoln—then to my unpleasant realization, he turns into the Cattlemen's batwings of the saloon before he is near enough to hail. The fact is, the last place I want to confront him is on a public street or in a public restaurant or saloon.

I need his undivided attention, not him yelling for help to apprehend a wanted man...me.

Revenge of the Damned

It's time to relax and roll with the blows. There's a well-covered walkway across from the Cattlemen's, and it's beginning to sprinkle so I cross over and find a bench outside of Mayberry's Mercantile, plop down, and pull my hat down low. The odors coming from the Cattlemen's, known for its generous beefsteaks, are making my stomach talk back to me. But my mission is more important than quieting my growling gut with supper.

A dozen or more come and go from the dining room, until, finally, a distinguished looking man in a top hat exits. It's been more than a half dozen years since I've seen General, now Judge, Peabody, and this man seems a little heavier and his step not as stride-military like, but he already had gray hair although then only in his forties, and this man has tufts of gray showing under his high hat.

I rise and angle across the street to catch up. I had hopes of confronting him in his boarding house room, but the street is nearly vacant and I'm growing impatient. When only a have dozen paces behind, I call out, "General! General Peabody!"

He stops and turns, and eyes me carefully, but without recognition. "It's Judge Peabody now, sir. But, yes, it was general. Did you serve under me?"

"No, sir, but I've met you. May I walk along?"

"I'm hurrying as it appears the sky will open up...but if you don't mind a brisk pace—"

"We had to keep one to match that of Sherman."

"So you did."

He sets out again. "I've got three more blocks."

I pull the medal from my pocket and hold it out so he can see. "You presented this to me, sir."

"I did, did I? I presented or was beside the president for the presentation of four of those, two under Lincoln, one beside Johnson, and one beside Grant. If you're the recipient of one, then I'm proud to walk with you."

"Thank you, but I have a favor to ask of you."

"Paddy's is in the next block. I'd be happy to stand you to a nightcap and we can talk there."

"Suits me, but I should stand you—"

"Wouldn't think of it. My treat anytime to a man of such honor."

We got settled at a table near the rear of the place, and I'm happy to note there are fewer than a dozen customers, the bartender, and only one barmaid. The piano player must have the night off, which pleases me as we can hear each other.

So, I face it head on, "Judge, I'm Lincoln Dolan, and Marshal Wentworth is a lying son of a bitch and is getting away with the murder of his wife…my former fiancé."

Chapter Forty Eight

THE JUDGE LEANS BACK in his seat and stares at me. "I thought that name was familiar. I presented you with that medal in a military hospital in Carolina, if I recall correctly. Lincoln went to Virginia just as Grant was preparing to attack Lee's lines around Petersburg and Richmond, an assault we hoped would end the siege that had dragged on for many months. Sherman's force was damn near at a run northward through the Carolinas. For the first time, Lincoln and Sherman met at Grant's City Point headquarters at the general-in-chief's request. It was a momentous occasion. And you're the fellow on the poster."

"All true, but I'm mostly the innocent fellow on the poster. I walked out of the Cattlemen's and had half the town throwing lead all around me. Hit me in the side, hit me in the thigh. I fired back at fellas shooting at me, as any sane man would. In my eyes that's self-defense."

"You hit Johnny Fellows in the hip and knocked him off his horse as I get the story. He's a nice young man who'll walk with a limp the rest of his days."

"He did not present his credentials to me, Judge, unless you consider .44 slugs flying all around me, hitting me twice, killing my horse, his credentials. I did relieve the hitching rail of another animal, a fine dun which I'm willing to return or pay for, either way."

Our drinks arrive and he takes a long draw on the brandy he's ordered, not taking his eyes off me. "So, what's this about Wentworth?"

"His deputy...former deputy...Dob, is a guest, an unwilling guest, but a guest, where I'm hanging my hat of late. As are a couple of fellas who claim to be deputies...Guzman and McCallester. Dob and I have had a couple of long talks, and he informs me that Wentworth threatened him if he didn't lie about the death of Maggie Mae, his wife."

"He lied?"

"He lied. Maggie Mae did not come at him as Dob testified. She was unarmed. Wentworth killed her in cold blood—"

"Dob said that?"

"Well, no sir. Dob said that he was forced to lie that he saw Maggie come at Wentworth. Why would Wentworth coerce Dob to lie if the lie was unnecessary?"

"You sound like an attorney, Mister Dolan." The judge says, and smiles, if slightly.

"Hardly, sir. I'm just a man whose been wronged, but not nearly so wronged as an innocent young woman who was as kind and loving—"

"Loving in a carnal way, with you, as the rumor goes."

"I'm not proud of that, sir, although I admit I'd often dreamed of the act. Wentworth lied to her. She was promised to me and I returned from the war to find her married to the bastard...he was known to his men as Wentworthless...and it was more than a half dozen years gone by when I ran into them here in town. Maggie was shocked that I wasn't dead. It seems Wentworth said he saw me killed and buried on the field of battle, so she would think it so and be free to marry that bastard. He knew damned well I wasn't dead. She came to my room, I didn't seek her out...and yes, she was a married woman, but as God is my witness she should have been married to me and in the eyes of the Lord she consummated that marriage upstairs in the Cattlemen's...and died for it."

He rubs his chin in a thoughtful way, then reaches in a waistcoat pocket and removes a pair of pince nez eyeglasses and adjusts them on his nose. Then he looks at me over the top of them in a serious way that says to me he is about to pass judgment.

"Mister Dolan, receiving that medal doesn't make you, or mean you to be, an honest man. It respects your bravery, but there's been many a man who's been brave outside the law. That said, I think you're telling me the truth. The fact is I've had past experiences with Wentworth and nothing he's ever done would make me doubt what you're saying. You should turn yourself in. We'll get Dob back here and—"

I glance up and my look stops the judge short from trying to convince me. Wentworth is standing at the bar facing us. His right hand rests on the revolver on his hip and he is reaching across the bar with his left to receive a sawed-off scattergun handed him by the bartender. And the bartender is pulling a small revolver from his waistband in the same motion. Another deputy stands slightly behind the big Marshal, and he, too, is pulling a hog leg from a low-slung holster.

Wentworth swings the muzzles our way, cocking both barrels at the same time.

I flip the table over, sending drinks flying, and lunge at the judge, shoving him sprawling on the floor. He hasn't see Wentworth and his eyes flare wide and he yells, "What the..."

But the yell is cut short by the roar of both barrels as the table top explodes with two dozen holes just when I hit the floor. I roll and rise to a crouch, running for a rear door. The door jamb spits splinters and I presume the bartender and deputy have joined the fray with their pistols.

The last impression I have before I make my way down the hall at a dead run is the judge, bloodied and on his back on the barroom floor.

A sawed-off scattergun at twenty paces, likely loaded with cut up square nails, is damned indiscriminate about who it bloodies.

I burst into an alleyway as dark as a foot up a buffalo's butt, and run. Then wipe at my neck and face and realize I, too, am bleeding.

Chapter Forty Nine

I'M SURE THEY THINK I'M pounding trail out of town, but I've not finished my errand, in fact, I've just begun. I have a gouge on my neck and one on my cheek. I'm not going to be any more handsome, but then again I can't remember worrying about it. I have the bleeding stopped in short order.

If the judge is shot dead I'm sure I'll be blamed. If he's only wounded I'm sure he'll be cognizant of the fact I was not the one got him shot and it was the fool who fired a weapon that likely spread ten feet at twenty paces. The fellow who was responsible, Wentworth, didn't give a damn who got shot so long as I got the worst of it.

So, in the darkness, I gather up my dun and lead him back to a hitching rail at the rear of the mercantile and take up my perch in the deep shadow of the porch across from the front of the Cattlemen's and watch.

A crowd has gathered in the Cattlemen's saloon, mostly from the restaurant next door but I'm sure some from the street. In my absence to bring my mount closer, in case I must flee in a hurry, a doctor has come on the scene. I presume that as I see a nicely dressed fella in a citified bowler hat carrying a back bag exit the bar, and he wasn't there when the trouble occurred. I'm happy to note it's not the undertaker taking his leave with a couple of fellas carrying the judge out on a slab.

It's not long after a half dozen make their way out that Wentworth and his deputy stomp out behind them. It seems Wentworth has a steam up as he's swinging his arms and giving the deputy next to him hell. They move off down the road.

The affair must have worked up a thirst for the judge, as it's another half hour before he walks out, a white bandage around his neck and he's carrying his coat and hat in one hand as the other arm is in an equally white sling.

He must be only two blocks from his boarding house, as he said three blocks when I met him just after leaving the Cattlemen's saloon, and I'd join him but a short dumpy fellow has taken it upon himself to escort the judge to his abode.

I let them get a block ahead, and there being no one else on the street, follow.

Waiting until the dumpy fellow takes his leave, after a short time, I wander up and walk right into Mrs. Crutchfield's Boarding House as if I'm a resident. There are a couple of fellows in front of the fire in a sitting room, playing cards, but they pay me little attention. I mount the stairs to the second floor and only one door has light in the crack at its bottom, so I stride right up and rap on it.

"Enter, if you can abide a man ready for his bed," the voice rings out and I'm sure it's the judge, so I do.

His eyes widen upon seeing me. "Well, Mr. Dolan, you're brazen if nothing else," he says, already in his nightshirt, his arm hanging at his side out of the sling but bandaged.

"We didn't have a chance to finish our talk, judge."

"And we're damn lucky to be able to talk at all, under the circumstance."

I laugh quietly. "It seems the good Marshal cared little about who got holed in his eagerness to dispatch yours truly."

"Don't think I didn't notice," the judge said raising a hand and covering the bandage on his neck. "The doc said another inch and a half and this neck wound would have been my undoing."

"And the arm?" I ask.

"Didn't get the bone. He said to wear the sling for a few days so it heals without a problem. It was through and through and the swab he followed the projectile with was an act to wake one right up, and the whiskey they poured on both wounds...let's just say I've had more enjoyment drinking the distilled nectar than using it as a dressing."

"I'm sorry, your honor. Had I not been—"

"Mister Dolan, we can't account for every fool in the world, but we can try and make sure some of them don't hurt anyone else. Now tell me all you know about this affair with Wentworth and his former wife."

The judge listens patiently as I go through all I know and all I've been told by Dob and declare I'd be remiss if I didn't try and rectify the situation. When I run out of steam, he stands and after replacing his bad arm in its sling, moves over and puts his good hand on my shoulder.

"Linc, there's no question in my mind that Wentworth...and I'll deny it if you repeat me...is worthless as tits on a boar. We had a dozen complaints against the colonel from his troops, accusing him of damn near every wrong in the book. But the war was over and all of us wanted to get on with the peace, so that was that. However, this is another opportunity to put things right. You go on back up the mountain. You make sure this Dob fellow comes to me. Tell him I can exempt him from prosecution if all he's done is ride out of town with a livery horse and a few supplies on the town's account. And with his testimony, we'll bring charges against Wentworth for his wife's murder. And the black...Bama, you call him. Mrs. Stanley has already spoken on his behalf and we've been pulling his posters off tree and rail."

I'm not convinced. "Most every man of standing in Helena is indebted to Wentworth. So, don't count on a Helena jury to convict the man."

"To hell with a Helena jury. I can change the venue to Bozeman or Fort Benton. You've got to get this Dob back here."

I shook my head in concern. "He's tied up in the barn, and talking like a Dutch uncle, but we think he's done more than he's admitting to. He came in with a woman, a mulatto lady from Junket City who's badly cut up and there's some talk around our camp that Dob was the dog who did it...but the woman hasn't accused him directly. She was running from something too."

"The proprietor of Maddie's in Junket City was shot by that woman, but it seems he's going to live. He'll not be right as she left a chunk of lead in his head, but he's alive. He wasn't well thought of and there's talk of him mistreating the woman, and other women. If he lives I'm sure that's the end of it."

"Then it's my task to get Dob back here in a talking mood?" I say, rubbing my chin.

"I'll give this Dob immunity for what he took when he left town. I have no knowledge of his cutting up the woman so I won't speak to that, nor will the decree of immunity cover that affair, if it happened. But he has to testify against Wentworth. If he does so, he'll walk free for stealing the horse and supplies."

I rise and extend my hand to Peabody. "Sir, I hope we can make this right and—"

Before I can finish the sentence, someone raps on the door, hard enough to make both Judge Peabody and me jump back.

Then a voice rings from behind the pounding, "By God, Judge, is that Dolan in there with you?"

It's Wentworth.

Chapter Fifty

"GET ON THE OTHER SIDE OF THE BED," I command the judge, in a tone that can't be ignored, while at the same time moving to put my back to the wall next to the hinge side of the paneled door.

The judge wastes no time and rolls across the top of the bed, and it's a good thing he does as the door is suddenly ventilated with three shots as fast as a man can pull off a single action.

"Wentworth!" the judge shouts, "you damn fool..."

But his voice is drowned by two shots from my Navy Colt, also fired through the door at two different angles.

"Oh, goddamned," Wentworth's voice now sounds fearful. Then footsteps disappear down the hallway. Not one man; at least two.

"You hit?" I ask the judge.

"No, and no thanks to Wentworth."

"I think I must have clipped him. Wish it had been between the eyes, but he's gone...I think."

"You need to get out of town...and bring Dob back here."

"Judge, the Marshal must have overheard our conversation. He obviously didn't give a damn if you were hit or not. If so, he would have likely finished you off and blamed it on me."

"Makes sense," Peabody replies. "Only a madman would shoot through a door not knowing who he'd hit."

"Maybe you should come with me," I say.

"Bad idea, but a good idea is getting me to the Cattlemen's."

"He won't shoot you if they're witnesses?" I surmise.

"Probably not, but that's not my reasoning. Seth Paul Perkins, our new Federal Marshal just came in today and is staying there. Wentworth paled when I told him Perkins was taking up residence here, and hiring four deputies to work the territory." The judge speaks as he's getting dressed.

"They went out the front, let's go out the back?" I suggest.

The judge walks to his window, that looks out on a side yard where Mrs. Crutchfield kept a garden, now a stubble of dry sticks. "Can't see them, front or back."

"Do you have a firearm, sir?" I ask.

"In my drawer..." he says, and in a moment is strapping on a gun belt, holster, and small Sheriff's model Colt.

"Shall I flip a coin?" I ask.

"I say the back way. We can stay in the alley until we reach the Cattlemen's."

I reload my Navy and check the loads in the Henry. I'm loaded for bear, or for a bear-size Marshal.

Wishing I could say I was fit as a fiddle but the fact is after the ride down the mountain, my side has been paining me something terrible and I'm still a bit gimpy in the leg that lost a chunk to a bullet as I limp ahead of the judge to the back stairway.

"Did he hit you?" the judge asks from behind as we top the much smaller back stairway.

"No, sir. You're the only one of us with fresh blood. You doing okay?"

"Other than having my dander up, I'm doing fine. The more I think on it, the madder I get at Wentworth. It's almost as if he wants me dead."

"Wentworth doesn't give a damn who dies so long as he stays fat and sassy, and running Helena."

The house is dark and there's no light coming from the sitting room near the front door, so I ask the judge again. "You sure it's the back door?"

"Six one way, half a dozen the other," he says, and I understand the logic.

So, I head to the back door. "Let me go out first. I'd hate the territory to lose their federal judge before he has a chance to rule on his first case."

"Not so much as I'd hate it," he says, and flashes me a grin. You got to admire a man who doesn't lose his sense of humor even under the worst conditions.

I ease the door open, glad there's no backlight, and step out onto a step only as wide as the door, and thank God it is as my next step is off the side and I go headfirst into a lilac bush just as I catch the flash of a rifle from somewhere near the rear fence, twenty paces away. A propitious accident or I'd be a dead man.

I cock the Golden Boy as it comes to my shoulder and fire at the location of the muzzle flash. Then I scramble to the side, staying with my back against the wall, with the visual cover of a row of man-high lilac bushes in front of me, not that anyone could see me in the darkness.

As loud as I dare, I call out to the judge, "You hit, judge."

"No," he calls back. "Going out the front," he says, and I hear footfalls disappearing down the hall.

My eyes have adjusted to the dark, and to my pleasant surprise I see a small glow down the alley from the back fence, not more than forty paces from me. Then to the right ten feet from that glow, another rifle shoots flame and the back door to Mrs. Crutchfield's boarding house splinters as he fires two rapid shots.

I push through the bushes enough to get a clear bead on the glow, thinking the rifle could be a deputy who I have no interest in filling full of holes unless I absolutely have to, but the glow is likely the cigar of a fat Marshal. A bad habit in a night fight.

Firing at what I hope is a foot below the glow, about heart level, I let one fly then as fast as I can lever in, fire twice more, but high, where the last shots came from.

Before the echo of my shots die out, I hear caterwauling louder than a buffalo bull in heat, and a second voice yelling, "You hit, Oscar?"

But if so, not hard enough I decide as Wentworth's voice screams at his man, "You dumb bastard, you think I'm yelling 'cause I'm happy. Of course I'm hit. Keep that som'bitch pinned down while I get out of here."

I can't help but smile thinking I've hit the fat Marshal twice, likely once through the room door, and again now. He's a big target, and likely I merely cut a groove in a layer of fat, so I'm not bragging.

I've moved at least a dozen paces to my left and make out what can tell, mostly by feel, is a buggy, so I continue and round it using it for cover and make my way toward the alley. The second man fires again at the back of the house, doing as the Marshal instructed. He fires twice more, obviously caring little about who might be domiciled inside.

Then I hear the telltale sound of a hammer falling on an empty chamber.

It's time to take a risk, so I run as fast as my aching side and leg will allow. Twenty paces down the alley I come upon a tall, skinny fellow trying to jam cartridges into his Winchester.

He looks up and yelps just as the butt of my Yellow Boy slams into his face. He goes over backwards, hits flat, and spins to his belly, trying to crab away. But I'm on him like hair on a hog and this time the butt of the rifle clunks into the back of his head. He's face first in the mud so I take a moment to turn his head to the side. Hate to have a fella's mother learn he smothered to death in a pile of horse apples.

I hear some yelling a block away, and someone pounding on a door. So, crow hopping down the alley, I head toward the sound.

Crossing a side-street I continue into the alley on the other side, and slow as I am, I'm close enough I can make out what he's yelling and know I'm again dealing with an armed man.

"Damn it, Felix, let me in. I'm bleeding out here."

I doubt if anyone other than Oscar Wentworth would be bleeding in an alley so I head straight toward the voice.

Then the door opens and light floods my target.

Chapter Fifty One

I'VE SHOT MEN NOT LOOKING at me or knowing I was in the neighborhood, but that was war and this is far more personal. With the Golden Boy shouldered, I yell at Wentworth, "Hey, you fat woman killing son of a bitch, where do you want it?"

He spins and raises his sidearm, but fires way too fast and likely at the voice as I'm sure he can't see me. His shot flies wild. I guess I'm distracted as there are footfalls coming down the side yard, and more than one man.

I drop to one knee and snap a shot off at Wentworth before he can disappear inside the house. He screams like a little girl and tumbles off the porch, and whoever is inside slams the door.

"Dolan, that's enough," a voice rings out and it's the judge. "I've got Seth Perkins, the Territorial Federal Marshal here. This is over."

The heat floods my backbone as it's not over for me. "I'm backing out of here, Judge. I won't go to jail over this no-good woman killing bastard."

"Lay down your weapons. You have my word you can fetch your witness and we'll have a hearing. If things are as you say, all you've done is in self-defense."

"I'll lay them down, but I'm taking them back up the mountain with me."

"Just set them aside. It'll make Seth a little more comfortable. Let's see how bad Wentworth is hit."

Taking the judge at his word, I place the Henry and my Remington down, and yell, "Weapons are on the ground, judge. Don't make me sorry I'm trusting you."

***

As I'd hoped, Judge Peabody, formerly General Peabody, was a man of his word.

Unfortunately Wentworth was not shot dead, but creased on the side, a gouge cut in a bicep, and my last shot holed his upper leg and busted it all to hell.

And the hell of it is, he didn't bleed to death. But with one leg likely shorter than the other he'll walk in circles the rest of his stinkin' life. If he doesn't hang before it heals.

I got Dob back to town and with Judge Peabody presiding, my hearing went well and I was exonerated, except for having to pay some damages to the deputy I shot when fleeing town when Wentworth first came after me. I bought him a fine new saddle horse, as I'd killed the one he was riding. And I returned the dun to its rightful owner.

Then came Wentworth's pre-trial hearing. Anyone else would have hung, but as it was, him being City Marshal and all, he was given ten years in the federal lockup. I pray he'll come after me when and if he gets out. However, some Lawmen don't always fare well in the pen. With luck, his fellow inmates will mete out justice.

Abby and I were married with Peabody doing the honors. Jed stood up as my best man and Marie 'Belle' Bellerose stood up with Abby. Then some places were switched and I stood up with Bama and Abby with Belle as the two of them became man and wife.

I wasn't surprised when we had to patch together a second wagon and they followed us out in the Spring.

Seems Bama and I have decided to go into the wagon building and saddle making business with my few dollars, five hundred that Belle has contributed, and another five hundred that Abby got for her homestead; a fine cabin, barn, and three hundred twenty acres of timber land.

We're going to ride west until the urge hits us to stake out a homestead, hopefully near a market for wagons and saddles. With two couples, we can lay claim to six hundred forty acres…a full section.

We've had lots of trouble. The good news is we ended up with a fairly new Sharps .45/.90, a fine pair of Percherons…and better yet, it turned out Wentworth had kept my hound, Scout. I got Scout back and he was hound-dog happy to see me.

A new beginning.

A Look at West of the War by L.J. Martin

Young Bradon McTavish watches the bluecoats brutally hang his father and destroy everything he's known, and he escapes their wrath into the gun smoke and blood of war. Captured and paroled, only if he'll head west of the war, he rides the river into the wilds of the new territory of Montana where savages and grizzlies await. He discovers new friends and old enemies...and a woman formerly forbidden to him. Action adventure at its best from the author of Nemesis, Mr. Pettigrew, the Montana Series, and many more acclaimed westerns and historicals.

About the Author

L. J. Martin is the author of over three dozen works of both fiction and non-fiction from Bantam, Avon, Pinnacle and his own Wolfpack Publishing. He lives in, and loves, Montana with his wife, NYT bestselling romantic suspense author Kat Martin. He's been a horse wrangler, cook as both avocation and vocation, volunteer firefighter, real estate broker, general contractor, appraiser, disaster evaluator for FEMA, and traveled a good part of the world, some in his own ketch. A hunter, fisherman, photographer, cook, father and grandfather, he's been car and plane wrecked, visited a number of jusgados and a road camp, and survived cancer twice. He carries a bail-enforcement, bounty hunter, shield. He knows about what he writes about, and tries to write about what he knows.

Other Fine Action Adventure from L. J. Martin

West of the War

Young Bradon McTavish watches the bluecoats brutally hang his father and destroy everything he's known, and he escapes their wrath into the gunsmoke and blood of war. Captured and paroled, only if he'll head west of the war, he rides the river into the wilds of the new territory of Montana where savages and grizzlies await. He discovers new friends and old enemies...and a woman formerly forbidden to him.

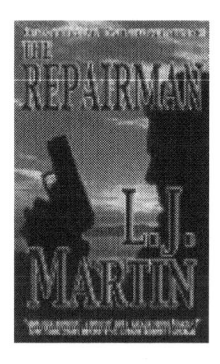

The Repairman. No. 1 on Amazon's crime list! Got a problem? Need it fixed? Call Mike Reardon, the repairman, just don't ask him how he'll get it done. Trained as a Recon Marine to search and destroy, he brings those skills to the tough streets of America's cities. If you like your stories spiced with fists, guns, and beautiful women, this is the fast paced novel for you.

The Bakken No. 1 on Amazon's crime list! The stand alone sequel to The Repairman. Mike Reardon gets a call from his old CO in Iraq, who's now a VP at an oil well service company in North America's hottest boomtown, and dope and prostitution is running wild and costing the company millions, and the cops are overwhelmed. If you have a problem, and want it fixed, call the repairman...just don't ask him what he's gonna do.

G5, Gee Whiz When a fifty million dollar G5 is stolen and flown out of the country, who you gonna call? If you have a problem, and want it fixed, call the repairman...just don't ask him what he's gonna do.

Who's On Top Mike Reardon thinks his new gig, finding an errant daughter of a NY billionaire will be a laydown...how wrong can one guy be? She's tied up with an eco-terrorist group, who proves to be much more than that. And this time, the group he's up against may be bad guys, or kids with their heart in the right place. Who gets lead and who gets a kick in the backside.

And if things go wrong, the whole country may be at risk! Another kick-ass Repairman Mike Reardon thriller from acclaimed author L. J. Martin.

Target Shy & Sexy   What's easier for a search and destroy guy than a simple bodyguard gig, particularly when the body being guarded is on of America's premiere country singers and the body is knockdown beautiful...until she's abducted while he's on his way to report for his new assignment. Who'd have guessed that the hunt for his employer would lead him into a nest of hard ass Albanians and he'd find himself between them and some bent nose boys from Vegas! Another in the highly acclaimed The Repairman Series...Mike Reardon is at it again.

Judge, Jury, Desert Fury. Back in the fray, only this time it's as a private contractor. Mike

Reardon and his buddies are hired to free a couple of American's held captive by a Taliban mullah, and, as usual, it's duck, dodge and kick ass when everyone in the country wants a piece of you. Don't miss this high action adventure by renowned author L. J. Martin. No. 6 in The Repairman series, each book stands alone.

No Good Deed. Going after some ruthless kidnappers, who want NATO,s secrets, is one thing...going into Russia is another altogether. But when one of Reardon's crew is being held, he says to hell with it, no matter if he's risking starting World War 3! Why not add the CIA and the State Department to your list of enemies when your most important job is staying alive hour by hour, minute by minute.

Overflow. Mike Reardon, the Repairman, hates to mess his own nest—to work anywhere near where he lives. If you can call a mini-storage and a camper living. But when terrorists bomb Vegas, and a casino owner's granddaughter is killed...the money is too good and the prey is among his most hated. Then again nothing is ever quite like it seems. Now all he has to do is stay alive, tough when friends become enemies and enemies far worse, and when you're on top the FBI and LVPD's list.

Quiet Ops. "...knows crime and how to write about it...you won't put this one down." Elmore Leonard

L. J. Martin with America's No. 1 bounty hunter, Bob Burton, brings action-adventure in double doses. From Malibu to West Palm Beach, Brad Benedick hooks 'em up and haul 'em in...in chains.

Crimson Hit. Dev Shannon loves his job, travels, makes good money, meets interesting people...then hauls them in cuffs and chains to justice. Only this time it's personal.

Bullet Blues. Shannon normally doesn't work in his hometown, but this time it's a friend who's gone missing, and he's got to help...if he can stay alive long enough. Tracking down a stolen yacht, which takes him all the way to Jamaica, he finds himself deep in the dirty underbelly of the drug trade.

Windfall. From the boardroom to the bedroom, David Drake has fought his way…nearly…to the top. From the jungles of Vietnam, to the vineyards of Napa, to the grit and grime of the California oil fields, he's clawed his way up. The only thing missing is the woman he's loved most of his life. Now, he's going to risk it all to win it all, or end up on the very bottom where he started. This business adventure-thriller will leave you breathless.

Bloodlines. When an ancient document is found deep under the streets of Manhattan, no one can anticipate the wild results. A businessman is forced to search deep into his past and reach back to those who once were wronged, and redeem for them what is right and just. There's a woman he's yearned for, and must have, but all is against them…and someone wants him dead.

The Clint Ryan Series:

El Lazo. John Clinton Ryan, young, fresh to the sea from Mystic, Connecticut, is shipwrecked on the California coast…and blamed for the catastrophe. Hunted by the hide, horn and tallow captains, he escapes into the world of the vaquero, and soon gains the name El Lazo, for his skill with the lasso. A classic western tale of action and adventure, and the start of the John Clinton Ryan, the Clint Ryan series.

Against the 7th Flag. Clint Ryan, now skilled with horse and reata, finds himself caught up in the war of California revolution, Manifest Destiny is on the march, and he's in the middle of the fray, with friends on one side and countrymen on the other…it's fight or be killed, but for whom?

The Devil's Bounty. On a trip to buy horses for his new ranch in the wilds of swampy Central California, Clint finds himself compelled to help a rich Californio don who's beautiful daughter has been kidnapped and hauled to the barracoons of the Barbary Coast. Thrown in among the Chinese tongs, Australian Sidney Ducks, and the dredges of the gold rush failures, he soon finds an ally in a slave, now a newly freedman, and it's gunsmoke and flashing blades to fight his way to free the senorita.

The Benicia Belle. Clint signs on as master-at-arms on a paddle wheeler plying the Sacramento from San Francisco to the gold fields. He's soon blackmailed by the boats owner and drawn to a woman as dangerous and beautiful as the sea he left behind. Framed for a crime he didn't commit, he has only one chance to exact a measure of justice and…revenge.

Shadow of the Grizzly. "Martin has produced a landlocked, Old West version of Peter Benchley's *Jaws*," Publisher's Weekly. When the Stokes brothers, the worst kind of meat hunters, stumble on Clint's horse ranch, they are looking to take what he has. A wounded griz is only trying to stay alive, but he's a horrible danger to man and beast. And it's Clint, and his crew, including a young boy, who face hell together.

Condor Canyon. On his way to Los Angeles, a pueblo of only one thousand, Clint is ambushed by a posse after the abductor of a young woman. Soon he finds himself trading his Colt and his skill for the horses he seeks...now if he can only stay alive to claim them.

The Montana Series – The Clan:

Stranahan. "A good solid fish-slinging gunslinging read," William W. Johnstone. Sam Stranahan's an honest man who finds himself on the wrong side of the law, and the law has their own version of right and wrong. He's on his way to find his brother, and walks into an explosive case of murder. He has to make sure justice is done...with or without the law.

McCreed's Law. Gone...a shipment of gold and a handful of passengers from the Transcontinental Railroad. Found...a man who knows the owlhoots and the Indians who are holding the passengers for ransom. When you want to catch outlaws, hire an outlaw...and get the hell out of the way.

Wolf Mountain. The McQuades are running cattle, while running from the tribes who are fresh from killing Custer, and they know no fear. They have a rare opportunity, to get a herd to Mile's and his troops at the mouth of the Tongue...or to die trying. And a beautiful woman and her father, of questionable background, who wander into camp look like a blessing, but trouble is close on their trail...as if the McQuades don't have trouble enough.

O'Rourke's Revenge. Surviving the notorious Yuma Prison should be enough trouble for any man...but Ryan O'Rourke is not just any man. He wants blood, the blood of those who framed him for a crime he didn't commit. He plans to extract revenge, if it costs him all he has left, which is less than nothing...except his very life.

McKeag's Mountain. Old Bertoldus Prager has long wanted McKeag's Mountain, the Lucky Seven Ranch his father had built, and seven hired guns tried to take it the hard way, leaving Dan McKeag for dead...but he's a McKeag, and clings to life. They should have made sure...for now it will cost them all, or he'll die trying, and Prager's in his sights as well.

The Nemesis Series:

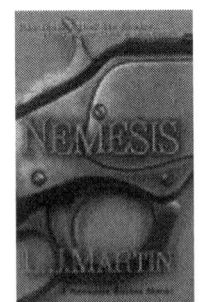

Nemesis. The fools killed his family…then made him a lawman! There are times when it pays not to be known, for if they had, they'd have killed him on the spot. He hadn't seen his sister since before the war, and never met her husband and two young daughters…but when he heard they'd been murdered, it was time to come down out of the high country and scatter the country with blood and guts.

Mr. Pettigrew. Beau Boone, starving, half a left leg, at the end of his rope, falls off the train in the hell-on-wheels town of Nemesis. But Mr. Pettigrew intervenes. Beau owes him, but does he owe him his very life? Can a one-legged man sit shotgun in one of the toughest saloons on the Transcontinental. He can, if he doesn't have anything to lose.

The Ned Cody Series:

Buckshot. Young Ned Cody takes the job as City Marshal…after all, he's from a long line of lawmen. But they didn't face a corrupt sheriff and his half-dozen hard deputies, a half-Mexican half-Indian killer, and a town who thinks he could never do the job.

Mojave Showdown. Ned Cody goes far out of his jurisdiction when one of his deputies is hauled into the hell's fire of the Mojave Desert by a tattooed Indian who could track a deer fly and live on his leavings. He's the toughest of the tough, and the Mojave has produced the worst. It's ride into the jaws of hell, and don't worry about coming back.

Revenge of the Damned